Wreck Me

by

J. L. Mac

Amy!
Thanks for reading!
XO
J L Mac

Dedication

For my readers.

Your support and enthusiasm humbles me.

Table of Contents

Prologue

Saturday, June 8th, 1996

I love this car. It smells so good. Papa just got it for us and Maman won't let me eat or drink anything in it like I did in the other one. Maman says it's cause it's our first *nouvelle voiture*. She always tells me that it's our first new car in French and she makes her words sound all fancy. I think she does it to make me laugh. I like it when Maman uses French instead of English because she always uses her fancy voice. Papa scolds her when she does that. He says "Collette, you hinder our darling girl only speaking French. English, *mon amour*, English." He only pretends to fuss at Maman. I know this because after he scolds her, he always does this winky thing with his eye and Maman smiles at him.

I can hardly wait for the carnival. It's only here for two days and my best friend, Michelle, is going. Her parents are taking her today, too. I hope I will get to see

1

her there. "How much longer, Maman?" I know I asked only a minute ago but I am too excited to wait much longer.

"Josephine, *de quelques minutes*." I know I shouldn't whine. Papa says I'm too old to whine like a little kid. He says a nine-year-old girl has no business acting like a baby. But I can't help it. I want to be there already. The rides have long lines and it will take forever to take a turn on all of them.

"Maman, how many minutes is a few?"

Papa is looking at me in the mirror and I know he's telling me to stop whining. I smile at him. It always makes him happy when I smile. He does the winky thing with his eyes and I know I'm not in any trouble. Papa is talking to Maman about grown up stuff. I'm not listening. It's too boring. Papa says a swear word and I know something is wrong.

"Papa!" He isn't answering me. *Ouch!* I hurt all over. "Maman!" I'm crying now. This hurts so badly and I'm scared. Maman and Papa aren't saying anything. *Are they hurt?* "Help! Someone help us!" I hope someone hears me screaming. I'm stuck in the backseat. I'm trying to get free, but my leg hurts so much I'm scared to move it again. "Help!" I still don't hear anything from Maman and Papa in the front seat. I feel something warm on my leg and look down. "Please!" I'm really scared now. There's blood all over the car. There's blood coming from Maman's head. Papa is slumped in front of me; I still can't see him. I'm stuck behind his seat. Our new car is ruined. It's all crumpled, like one of the empty soda cans I always smash. I hear something. I try to stop crying so I can hear better.

"Oh, God. Oh, God. I'm so sorry. Oh, God." It's a man. No, he's a boy. Maybe he's just a big boy. High school. Yeah, definitely a high school boy.

"Please, help me!" I cry out. I hope he gets me out of here without hurting me too much. Maman needs help. Her head is bleeding a lot. I don't think its okay for her to bleed that much.

"I've got you. C'mon. Dad, get them out of the front. GO!"

This boy is crazy. He just screamed at his dad. I would never talk to my mom and dad like that. I'd be grounded for a month. *Ouch!!* The big boy tugs open my door and reaches across to Maman. He picks up her wrist and holds his fingers by her pretty watch. Why is he doing that? He sets her hand back in her lap and drags me out of the back seat. It stinks in the street; it smells like something burning and gas. *Gross.*

"This is my fault. I'm sorry. I'm so sorry. I'll make sure you are okay."

I'm confused by the big boy. I don't know what to say. It's just a car. Maman and Papa will get another one. I just stare at him. My leg hurts. Michelle would make fun of me if she knew what I was thinking--*this big boy is kind of cute. He has pretty eyes for a boy.* The ambulance people are messing with me. They lift me onto one of those rolling bed things.

"What about my mom and dad? Where are they?" I sit up to look around for Papa and Maman, but I don't see them. The man in uniform that is taping wires to me won't answer me. I look over and see four people with matching uniforms on. They aren't policemen or firemen. They have rolling bed thingies like what I am on. *Here they come. They are helping Maman and Papa.* I don't feel so scared when I see the rolling beds go over to our new car. There are two men with each bed and I know they are getting Maman and Papa out of the wrecked car. Wait. This isn't right.

"Wait!" Why are they taking those beds on wheels somewhere else? Why not to me? Why can't I see them? Maman and Papa aren't moving or saying anything and I can't see their faces. I'm scared. Something isn't right. "Maman! Papa! Come back!" I'm getting really scared. I need to see them, to run to them, but the uniformed men aren't letting me go. They put these straps over me. I can't move; they won't budge. I feel something warm inside my arm where they put that needle thing. He called it an IV. My arm feels warm and now I'm getting sleepy. I feel like I'm moving and I want to ask where we're going, but my mouth won't work. I need to sleep. I close my eyes. I can ask questions later.

Chapter One

No Apologies

Friday, June 8th, 2012

I'm standing here, doing the same shit I do every year on this very day. But this just feels more crappy than normal. That isn't saying much, though, because complete crap is practically a staple in my life. Don't get me wrong, I lead a decent life. I work. I pay my taxes. My bills are paid on time. What little credit I have is good credit. I absolutely loathe my apartment and I may not have some plush, high-paying job, but all in all, my life is comfortable. God knows I've endured far worse. I refuse to complain about things.

Complaining is possibly the absolute most useless expenditure of energy known to mankind. I stopped complaining and feeling sorry for myself years ago when I realized exactly how useless it was. Complaining wasn't going to change my circumstances, so I said to hell with it and just quit. Now, I'm not trying to wear my shit life around like some badge of honor; I'm simply stating facts. No one knows my story; not even ass-wipe Sutton, and he's the only long term relationship I've got going. I keep it like that purely out of convenience. I don't like explaining the whole tragedy that is my life, and I damn sure don't feel like answering a million questions from some curious jerk-off. The last thing I expect, or want, is pity from others. I've had enough pity and condolences to last me two lifetimes.

I work hard to keep things organized and simple. My life hasn't always been so agreeable, and I'm not proud of my past. However, I can say with complete confidence that I did what I had to do out of necessity. I may have stolen food or a drink from a gas station a time or two, but I make no apologies for that. Did I pay for those items? No. I couldn't. I rarely had two pennies to rub together.

I stole those things out of the basic, fundamental, human need to survive. The alternative was starvation, and what human chooses morals and values over life? No one, that's who. Morals and values won't fill my stomach and hydrate my body, but stolen food and drink certainly will. I used the resources available to me on most days, but homeless kids are treated similarly to criminals. If I went to a shelter, I was usually tricked into staying put long enough so some lousy volunteer could call Social Services. Those schmucks would show up, I'd get crammed into the back of some government car and hauled off to a homeless kid's prison. It was really an orphanage, but a prison just the same.

The orphanage was usually far better than foster care. Well, in my experience that was the case. The folks at the orphanage were simply doing their job. They were earning their pay; they didn't care about us one way or another. If they didn't care enough to be kind and compassionate to us, they damn sure didn't care enough to waste time and energy on abusing or raping us unfortunate kiddies.

I preferred the people at the orphanage to all others, though it was always a short stay. They shuffled kids in and out of those doors just as quickly as they could.

After the orphanage, I was usually placed with some foster family who couldn't care less. All of this is done out of charity; out of obligation to do "the right thing." Is it really that damn difficult for people to see some kid on the street, even if that kid is better off fending for themselves there than in the crap place they came from? I suppose it messes with their heads and makes them all uncomfortable, so they'd rather those kids be placed somewhere out of sight and out of mind. That makes things easier for everyone, right? Wrong.

Back then, I preferred being on the streets instead of fighting off sexual abuse in one of the many foster homes I went through. I wish people would stop being so damn charitable. What these volunteers don't get is that their fucking charity causes more damage than people like me can bear. All for what? So that Suzy-Q, the once-a-month volunteer, can sleep better at night because she dished out crappy free soup to people like me. People who are "on hard times," who think they'd rather be dead than trudging through their shitty lives every day.

The least people like Suzy-Q can do, in my opinion, is be honest about things. Don't stand in front of some kid, who is exactly like I was, with pity written on your face and tell them life will work out, that things will start to look up for them, that one day their luck will change. That kind of bullshit does nothing but give false hope.

If my twenty-five-year-old self went back and met sixteen-year-old me, I would've looked myself in the face, with not one ounce of sadness, and said, "Look girl, you have a choice: you can stay like this and hope for all that bogus bullshit that people tell you to come true, or you can work your ass off and turn things around for yourself. No one is going to fix things for you. So get to it."

I refused to be a victim ever again, so I made my

way through my teen years on the streets. At least out there, I was in charge of me. Kids like me don't usually last long. Most end up as junkies, prostitutes, behind bars, or dead. A few of us luck out and make it, but for the most part, life simply is not that damn wonderful. Maybe I get my determination and perseverance from my parents. They came to this country with essentially nothing.

My dad was a French chef and he and my mom came here from Paris. They came to Las Vegas while my mom was still pregnant with me. My dad was a fantastic chef and he got a job at one of the five-star restaurants in town. I was only nine when they died, so I have limited memories, but I do remember that they were pretty driven people. I like to think that my ability to push forward with my life came from them, not from the years I spent avoiding rape on the streets and scavenging for food to avoid starving. I like to think that I come by my ambition honestly. In truth, no one will know for sure. They're dead and my few memories fade more with each passing day.

I always do this on this day; every damn year. It's exhausting, really. I'd rather not think about my life and how things have turned out, but the anniversary of the accident always stirs up the past. Those particles seem to stay suspended in the waters of my mind for a day or two, and then I manage to clear the murk and lock it all away where it belongs. For another 364 days.

I stop staring mindlessly at myself in the bathroom mirror and drag my weary ass out the door to partake in my normal routine. Stop by The Diner, order coffee and a bagel from Noni, head into work to deal with another day. It's always the same routine, and work is work.

I know that joker in the corner is up to no good; he has shady written all over him. I know the type. I used to be that type. I've made sure to watch him since he walked into the store. I like my job and I want to keep it, but people like him make the prospect of being unemployed in the near future all the more real. We're so far away from being in the black it's sickening. We're supposed to be selling books, but it seems no one is reading printed books anymore. Technology has been a selfish, monopolizing bitch. Sutton's ancient ass was in here this morning, moaning and groaning about not turning a decent profit since 1979 or some garbage. I wasn't really listening. He likes to come into the store and bicker about things, but he would be up shit creek without a paddle if it weren't for me.

I have single-handedly run this place for years, a one-woman staff in this old store. I landed this job seven years ago and haven't left since. He's a real piece of work, that Sutton. If I ever decided to quit I'd make sure to plant my foot square in his old ass on my way out. Truth is, I love this damn store way more than even Sutton does. I dread the day that I don't get to walk in and be greeted by the smell of ink and paper. I've come to depend on the hordes of authors who bled a portion of their souls onto paper for others to enjoy. Every book on these shelves is a friend. They are one of the very few mainstays in my life.

"Hey, bud. Can I help you?"

This guy just stuffed a book inside his disgusting sweater. That book costs a whopping four dollars and ninety-nine cents and he wants to steal it. What an asshole! Who the hell steals a book that costs less than five bucks? Who the hell steals a book in general?

"Hey, I asked you a question. Oh, hell no! Come back!" I take off running after the joker. He hauls ass for the exit and I scramble behind him.

He trips on the rug at the door and crashes into a tacky display of trinkets that Sutton insisted on putting out.

"HA! I'll take that, thank you very much!" I snatch the book from under his sweater and he makes a run for it, scurrying out of the store. I let him go. He's obviously homeless. Entertainment is limited for the unfortunate. I kneel on the floor with the recovered book in my grips, dusting it off and doing my best to straighten the creased corners my scuffle with the thief caused.

"Ahem."

I shoot to my feet and whirl around to see a man standing in the entrance to the store. The sun is still low in the morning sky and the rays of light pouring in behind the man are so bright I can't see him clearly.

"Are you all right, ma'am? I saw someone running out of here."

"Jo. My name is Jo. 'Ma'am' carries an implication of being something I'm not. So yeah, just call me Jo." I'm busy gathering the shit that's scattered all over the place thanks to my scuffle with the thief. The man squats down to pick up tacky trinkets and I get my first look at him. Hello, Greek god of all things masculine and sexy.

"An implication of what, exactly?" His voice is all curious and velvety.

I shrug my shoulders and try my best to get to the point so this cat will either show some interest or leave me the hell alone in my floundering bookstore. I prefer the former.

"You know... someone who's married or someone who's older, or someone who has stature or some type of title; someone who deserves respect. I'm none of that, so call me Jo." Why the fuck am I explaining my preference to this guy? His voice. Now that I think about it, it seems familiar for some reason. I'm sure I don't know this guy. It isn't possible. I don't have any friends whatsoever. I never have, really. Well, I had one friend, once upon a time. Michelle was my friend when I was a kid but I haven't had anyone since her.

"Okay. Jo."

"And you are?" I don't really give a shit, beyond the need to appease my own confusing sense of familiarity. I stop picking things up and look at him. His face seems familiar. Who the hell is this guy?

"Damon. Damon Cole." He extends his big paw and takes my hand in his.

The moment we touch, something floods through me and I don't have the slightest idea what the hell it is. Recognition? Arousal? I'm no stranger to a good looking man, and this man is for sure good looking. Most people would call me a slut, promiscuous at the very least. I think my sex life is the type of sex life most woman wish they'd indulge in but refuse to, since society as a whole frowns upon it. I stare curiously at him, our hands locked in a friendly shake.

"Do I know you?"

Mr. Handsome and Mysterious cocks his head to the side and surveys me speculatively. A tinge of pink has surfaced on his cheeks. Ah-ha! He is attracted to me too. I think I could live with a casual one night stand with this particular male specimen.

"No, Jo. I don't think so."

The way he says my preferred name has me thinking about all the naughty things I could do to him, given the chance of a hook up. I don't do the relationship thing, but I like sex just as much as the next person. Despite my aversion to lasting relationships of any sort, I get laid plenty.

"Did you come in here to buy something, Damon Cole, or was it the damsel in distress thing that lured you in?" I smile at the handsome man before me and wait to see if he takes the bait.

He does. "I didn't intend on purchasing a book, but if you'd like me to, I will."

I smile a devilish smile that I pray communicates what I'm thinking. I'm glad to help out Damon, but not with a book.

He narrows his eyes slightly, as if he's contemplating my subliminal offer. "Listen, I was headed to get some coffee, could you escape work for a few minutes to join me?"

I peek at my mother's watch on my wrist and smile. I can sneak an early lunch break. Sutton won't know, and even if he did, he likely wouldn't give a shit. Besides, what's he going to do, fire me?

"Okay, let's go."

The strange man smiles and it sets my insides into a sort of feeding frenzy. I can just imagine those lips of his pressed against my skin. I haven't had a man in weeks and he's going to be the perfect distraction from the anniversary of the accident and my looming unemployment. Yeah, I think I'll have him tonight.

We set out down the sidewalk to the café just down the block. I thank God that it isn't too hot out yet. June in Vegas is hellish. We stroll casually and alternate taking quizzical glances at each other. I take in the full view of him.

He wears the dress slacks like they were made for him, the sleeves of his dress shirt are rolled up his forearms, the top buttons are undone and he's without a tie. I bet he hates wearing those stuffy clothes, simply based on how casual he's made them. He's easily six feet tall, maybe more. His hair is slightly long on top but short on the sides and is the darkest of browns, edging toward black. He has a short, perfectly groomed beard across his angular jaw that I'm dying to feel against my cheek. His eyes glow in the sunlight like amber. His lips look soft and inviting and tilt up on just one side when he smiles. I can only imagine what's hidden beneath his clothes. I intend on finding out later.

He starts up the small talk as we take our coffee to a bistro table so small it feels instantly intimate. I like where this is going...

"So, you work at that bookstore alone?"

I give my coffee a swirl and set the wooden stirrer aside. I look up at the man across from me. God, he's gorgeous. I can't wait until tonight. I cut to the chase and go in for the kill. "Do you want to hang out tonight?"

His brows rocket up his forehead and I swear they met his hairline for a count. "Isn't that my line?"

I shrug. "I don't know, is it?"

He smiles back and his pearly whites make me melt. "It is. What time suits you?"

He's absentmindedly stirring his coffee in a slow constant rhythm and I watch the flick and swish of his wrist. I wonder if he moves that fluidly in bed.

"Sutton, the store owner, is coming in after lunch so then I'll leave. I have somewhere to be this afternoon, but I'll be free afterward. Want to meet me in front of the store around six?"

"Where do you have to be?"

Wow, he's pretty forward, isn't he? It's no damn business of his, but I'll teach him a quick lesson about a disease called foot-in-mouth-itis. It's a lesson I love handing out to people who pry.

"I'm going to the cemetery to visit my dead family," I say flatly.

Ha! There it is. Concern has filled his amber colored eyes.

"I apolog-"

This should be good. I hold up my hand to stop him; I have zero interest in apologies. They peeve me, in fact. They're almost never sincere. It's part of the human condition and one that I've never understood. What the hell is with the need to apologize? This man doesn't possibly feel sorry for my tragic scenario. I have no doubt that he feels sorry, but it isn't for me. It's for the embarrassment he feels for opening his mouth. He's sorry for himself, not for me.

"Don't. Don't apologize."

He snaps his lips shut and looks confused. It's actually a tad endearing. I kind of feel bad for tossing him under the bus. Hmm, that's an odd thing to feel. I actually feel a bit bitchy. This is so out of character for me. Well, what the hell do I say now? I didn't anticipate feeling like an asshole.

"Don't look at me like that. I just don't care for apologies. They're never sincere. I can vouch for this, since I have the urge at this very moment to say I'm sorry for being so rude. But honestly, my impulse to apologize is only because I feel uncomfortable with the guilt I feel and my stupid human brain associates an apology with mollifying my own discomfort. Apologies are just a reminder of how selfish people are." I let out an exasperated sigh. I chance a quick glance up at Damon and his eyes are glued to me.

"That is the most honest thing I think I have ever heard."

"I have to get back to the store. I'll meet you there at six?" I need to get away from this guy and forget about my own human conditions for the time being.

"Tonight at six," he confirms.

"Okay. Before I go..." I grab a napkin and dig a pen out of my bag. "Here's my number and email address in case you want to get in touch with me." I hand him the napkin and pause for a moment while he surveys the chicken scratches.

"jojo.geroux?" He looks confused.

"Josephine Geroux. That's my name. jo.geroux wasn't available so I went with jojo.geroux."

He just looks at me with the most peculiar look on his face and that deep feeling of familiarity surfaces again.

"See you tonight, Damon."

"Bye, Jo." His focus remains on the stupid napkin in

his hand as he mumbles his goodbye.

I stand and turn in my strappy sandals, point my frustrated self in the direction of the store, and allow my jean clad legs to carry me back to work as fast as they can.

Chapter Two

Perpetual Twilight

I was glad that my day flew by, but now that I see my parents' headstones come into view, I'm beginning to wish my day had crawled. The lump in my throat is growing with each step toward their final resting place. I fucking hate coming here. I only visit them once a year, on the anniversary of the accident. I can scrap in the streets, I can throw a perfect left hook, and when I had it, I could turn five bucks into fifty in no time, throwing dice in the alley. But damn, I can't get my shit together enough to visit my dead parents more than once a year. I'm a lousy daughter for it, but I tell myself that maybe they would understand my serious lack of intestinal fortitude when it comes to visiting their graves. I damn sure hope they understand, wherever they are. I like to think they're in heaven, but I just don't know. I have no way to know if it even exists, and the priest at the mission used to say I had to have faith that God and heaven are real. To a homeless teenager, the idea of having faith in anything is just asinine.

"Hi," I mumble as I kneel. These two stones are the only things, other than me, that attest to the existence of these two human beings. This is all that's left of them; two highly expensive grave markers that took a year's worth of savings for me to finally buy and of course, me, the product of their love. That's it. Nothing more. It claws at my hardened heart to know that Maman and Papa are reduced to this; two stones and a lousy daughter who never visits. I shake my head and purse my lips. My head seems to voluntarily hang in shame.

"I'm sorry," I croak out through welling tears. "I'm so sorry." My shoulders rock and I let the tears fall, unabashed. "I miss you. I miss you both so much it hurts to breathe. If I could, I would give all I have to bring you back." Like a real lady, I use the hem of my shirt to wipe at my sodden nose and cheeks. It really makes no difference. The tears still roll freely down my face to gather at the point of my chin before dripping to my lap. I don't give a shit. I'm hurting and I can't stop it. I miss them so damn much; some days it takes every ounce of strength to even exist.

Some days, the despair I feel threatens to drown me and that's a very dangerous kind of despair to muddle through. It's that kind of despair that makes people do stupid things just to gain a measure of relief from their suffering. I am ashamed to admit that I've contemplated ending it all. I know it's the selfish, cowardly thing to do, but the only fucking reason I've refrained from ending my shit life is because I would never want to disappoint my parents. I don't know if they can see or hear me, but I won't risk it. Living it is.

They didn't choose the way things ended up. The decision was made for them when that car veered into our lane. I could never disgrace them by pissing on the life they gave me. I'm all that remains of them besides these two stones, and I can't end them by ending myself. I brush away the dead grass that's scattered at the base of their markers. I trace my fingertips over the lettering on the heavily engraved stones; first his stone, then hers. I bought them once I'd saved enough money working at the store. I was nine years late, but my parents finally got the headstones they deserved, instead of the cheap plaque they had before. Most eighteen-year-old girls save for cars or an apartment of their own. I scrounged to buy my parents decent grave markers. I didn't give a shit that I ate next to nothing for that year while I stashed every penny I could. Knowing what my money was going towards was sustenance enough.

A growling stomach can be remedied; an ailing, broken heart cannot. I wish, somehow, there was something you could feed a broken heart to pacify it. Something I could do or have that would somehow lessen or alleviate the constant ache in my chest. I wondered and hoped for such a remedy, but the fact is, it doesn't exist. If it did, I would've already sought it out; I would've combed the planet for it. I would do anything to cure the void in me. So far, the only thing that seems to fill my emptiness is frequent, amazing sex. I guess I'm one of those textbook examples of a young woman using sex and promiscuity to distract from her shitty upbringing. I could care less. The sex is good and, for a short period of time, I forget everything.

"It doesn't feel any better. If anything, it hurts more. I wish I had something great to talk about, but I don't. I'm still at the store. I don't know how much longer, though. We may end up closing. I don't want to lose my job. It's all I've felt connected to since the accident." Tears build, spill over, and flow a little quicker with my talk of another loss. I can't stand the idea of not working at the store. It would just add to my sorrow. My job is all I have; it's all that I can look forward to. I'm content there. The thought of losing my beloved job makes me want to crumble. I spent countless hours in the library when I was on the streets and my love and appreciation for the written word runs deep. The words, the books, they've been my salvation.

People say time heals all wounds. I say those people are full of shit. Most people who are ignorant enough to say something so dumb have nothing to base that bullshit cliché on. There's no foundation of loss from which to draw that conclusion. I wouldn't dare tell someone who is grieving that time will heal them. I would be honest and say that time does nothing more than fade the good memories while building the void in your heart. The loss never dulls. I would tell someone grieving that the best they can hope for is that they find something productive to do to take the edge off. Any ambition of healing or any other hearts, rainbows and lollipops bullshit is just that; bullshit. When you suffer a loss so tremendous, it's like the sun goes down and never rises again. It sets and leaves you in a perpetual state of twilight.

I sniffle and wipe the tears away. "I love you both. Until next year." I stroke the pads of my fingers across their engraved names once more then pull myself to stand. I walk towards my car and thoughts of Damon Cole flood my mind. I more than want him now. I need him. I need to

cook?"

"No, not really." The admission leaves him a little embarrassed and damn if it isn't extremely cute seeing this tall, dark, handsome man looking flushed. His warm, amber eyes flit to the side, and for the first time since we saw each other, our gaze is broken.

"That's okay, I love to cook," I assure him. "If you're hungry, I'll make you dinner, but it'll have to be at your place. Mine is the crappiest apartment in this city."

A small smile eases across his mouth and his lips slant upward on one side. His confidence is back and his eyes practically gleaming with interest. He looks me up and down slowly, as if surveying my cooking ability. Between his adorable blush and those honey-colored eyes, he's winning all kinds of points with me. Damn, I want to put my mouth on him; on every single inch of him. I can feel heat growing in my cheeks and I know it's time to get this show on the road. "So......what do you say?" I ask with a coaxing smile. "Want me to wow you with my culinary skills or what?"

"I definitely want you to wow me, Jo. My car is this way."

Oh, for fuck's sake. This man is going to make sure I am begging for him. I can see it now. He knows what he has working in his favor and he is not afraid of showing it.

"No need. I'll follow you. Is your kitchen stocked?" I flip my keys once around my index finger and keep right on drinking in the sight of him. He still has one hand shoved in his pocket while the other dangles freely at his side. He nods his head in understanding.

"Okay, I get it. You don't really know me. But I promise you'll be okay. I'll make sure of it."

Something weird stirs within my subconscious; something familiar and frightening. My stomach turns sour in an instant and I feel like I should...do something. I don't know what the hell it is, but shit, this is a strange feeling. He must notice my discomfort because he steps forward and rests his hand on my upper arm.

"Hey, are you okay? Maybe you should let me drive. I promise to bring you back to your car the minute you tell me. Or, I can have it delivered to my place. My assistant won't mind. It's why I pay him."

"Uh, yeah, I'm fine. An assistant? He would bring my car, like, right now?" I arch an eyebrow in disbelief and he smiles and nods again.

His hand leaves my arm and he steps to my side, his hand taking up new residence at the small of my back, guiding me at a comfortable pace towards what I assume is his...pickup truck? He's pointing a key fob at a pickup truck of all things. This thing is lifted a bit, so getting into the passenger seat in my short denim skirt should be interesting.

"In you go."

In an instant, his hands are at my waist and he lifts me with ease, placing me into the passenger seat. I can't seem to form words. I'm fumbling around in my weary head for an answer. Maybe his car is being fixed. Maybe he's a serial killer and uses this pickup truck to transport bodies to the desert. Maybe he just likes trucks. Loads of men like trucks. It's the American man's vehicle of choice.

"Keys?" He holds out a hand to me while the other lifts his cell phone to his ear. I hand him my keys and listen to him speak. "Brian, yeah, I'll be back at my place in a few with my date. I need you to get a set of car keys with an address from security downstairs, then go pick up her car. It's a pale yell-, well... it's also got a red door, and a gray hood. You know what? I'll leave the plate number with the keys and you can find the car and bring it to my place. Yeah, thanks."

I can't help but laugh at his description of my crappy little car, a vehicle that looks more like a Franken-car than anything else. "Frank. It's my car's name."

He looks at me with disbelief written on his face. "You named your car? Why Frank?" He reaches in as he finishes his question and pulls the seatbelt out for me to buckle up.

"You know, Frankenstein car. She's all mad science looking, so I named her Frank." I shrug and smile.

He laughs as he shuts my door and makes his way around to the driver's side. It's one of those half smiles that seems to melt my panties right off and I have the urge to kiss him right here in his truck.

He hops in his seat and buckles his seatbelt. "Are you buckled in?"

I give my belt a tug to give him my answer and he starts his big man-toy of a truck. "Why in the world do you have wrist candy, yet drive a pickup truck?"

"Well, this is just one of my vehicles. I like to switch things up. I don't like getting bored or restless with only one car."

Definitely another ladies man having a good time on the playground known as Vegas. I can't blame him, though. I'm on the same damn playground. Of course, my scenario isn't as impressive; I don't sport a Rolex or a drive new car and my clothing sure isn't designer, but I make out just fine anyway.

"Okay, I get it. You like variety. Nothing wrong with that. Is your kitchen stocked or should we go to the store?"

"I think we can find something in my cabinets." He looks over to me and sends another panty-dissolving smile sailing my way and I soak it in. I could look at that smile all day.

The drive doesn't take long, and before I know it, we're at some seriously swanky high rise. It looks like typical Vegas high class.

"We're here," he says as he parks his nondescript pickup at this high class place.

I look to him and quirk up an eyebrow. "You're kidding, right? You live here?"

Damon doesn't respond. He slips out of the truck and walks around to open my door. It's a nice gesture; not many men do shit like that. I kind of like it. He reaches in and again grabs me about the waist and lifts me from the truck, pulling me to his rock solid body and slowly lowering me to my feet. Oh damn, this man smells and feels amazing. My heart speeds up and my breathing becomes rapid.

"Sorry. I didn't mean to be too forward."

"No need to apologize," I say, sounding a little breathy for my taste. "Shall we?" I nod and the alarm on his man-toy chirps as he locks it.

His hand finds the small of my back again and I revel in the warmth of his touch. He guides us into the foyer of the high rise building. This place is definitely swanky. What the hell does this guy do for a living? I will piss my pants if he says he owns a casino or some crazy shit like that. He's a little older than me. I can tell. How old is he? Thirties for sure. I'll ask later.

"How's it going, Howard?"

"Pretty good, Boss. What can I do for you?"

Damon slides my keys, chintzy rabbit foot keychain and all, across the security desk to Howard. "I need you to give these to Brian when he gets here, and this note." He grabs a pen and notepad from Howard's desk area and jots down my plate number. I catch the word "multi-colored" as he slips it back to the middle-aged Howard.

"Sure thing, Boss."

"Excuse me for being rude. Howard, this is my friend, Jo. Jo, this is Howard. He's Head of Security here at The Towers."

"Nice to meet you, Howard." I extend my hand to Howard and we shake.

"Likewise, ma'am."

"Please, just Jo. "

He releases my hand and smiles warmly. I like Howard. He seems like a cool guy.

"See you later, Howard," Damon tosses over his shoulder as he guides me towards a bank of elevators. Four, to be exact. Damn, this place is fancy. I feel uncomfortable. I don't want to touch a thing.

"You must be loaded to live in a place like this," I blurt before thinking better of it.

Damon chuckles and nods his head as we step into the elevator. The doors shut and he stamps a code into the control panel. We start to ascend the high rise.

"I'm an entrepreneur. I do well for myself."

It's a simple, vague explanation that leaves me curious to know more. The elevator has come to a halt and his hand on my back guides us through the elevator doors and into a foyer. He slides a panel open on the door and punches some buttons. I hear the click of a dead bolt. He opens the door and motions for me to walk ahead. I step into his private home and survey the space. It reeks of an overpriced interior decorator. Geez. This place is as "modern bachelor pad" as they come. It feels almost clinical, with all the clean lines and light color scheme. I can feel his eyes on me and I turn to face him. I nod and do my best to feign approval.

"You have a nice place. You must have had one of those expensive decorators huh?"

"Yeah. I paid her a considerable commission and she did this." He raises his hands and motions to the whole of our surroundings.

"You don't like it?"

"No, I guess I don't, but I'm not here much so it's

not that big of a deal."

"So make her change it! You paid her. You should be getting what you want." I fold my arms over my chest and scowl a bit. I have no reason to be annoyed over his shit, but I guess I have this deep rooted issue with people who fuck over others.

He cocks his head a fraction and studies me for a beat. "Come with me. I want to show you something."

I plop my purse down on the low profile couch and follow him. He leads us through the open space of his home, then up a flight of stairs. He keeps walking past the loft and I pause. Holy shit. Paradise. A loft library. He comes to stand beside me.

"Looks like your over-priced decorator either got something right or has multiple personalities." I stand perfectly still and admire the cozy library.

It's a huge contrast to the cold, modern theme that the rest of the penthouse is bathed in. This space is large by anyone's standards, but not on the same scale as the rest of his home. This loft feels smaller and cozier, like a place I could sit in for hours, reading book after book. It's amazing. There are only two walls in the loft, both of which are outfitted with floor to ceiling dark wood shelving. There must be thousands of books here. It's impressive. There are two oversized chairs that could easily be loveseats, upholstered in some fancy of fabric that reminds me of corduroy. They aren't leather and cold like the slim line furniture downstairs. The floor is carpeted, not tile or wood like the rest of the rooms. It feels plush, even through my sandals. I bet it feels great under bare feet. There's a coffee table and two end tables with small reading lamps on each. I notice that one of the walls has a few empty shelves. Why are they empty? I could fill those suckers up with my favorites. I make my way further into the loft and walk a slow path in front of one of the large bookshelves. I raise my fingers and allow them to lazily graze the spine of each book as I pass. The ink and paper smell like home to me.

"She didn't do the library or my bedroom. I handled both of them."

I turn away from the shelf and gape at him. "Wow." It's all I can force out. Damn, he just got way hotter in my opinion, and it's only because he has an obvious appreciation for books like I do. Maybe his appreciation is not quite like mine, but still.

He shows no clear response to my reaction. He makes his way to me and stops just in front of where I stand. His right hand lands on my shoulder and slips down the length of my arm until my fingers are tangled with his. "Come on."

I don't utter a fucking word because my heart is racing in my chest. Damn, the way he said that was sexy. He leads us from the loft. I look over my shoulder one more time at the most amazing private library I could ever imagine, then keep right on walking behind him. He swings open a door and walks me through it. I step into a room that is a world away from all things cold and clinical. This room feels plush. The walls are painted a neutral earth tone with one accent wall the color of sea water. His bed has a huge headboard that reminds me of one of those wingback chairs. It's upholstered and tufted and the fabric makes it look like it's bathed in champagne. He has two nightstands with lamps; there's a gas fireplace on the wall adjacent the bed. On the wall above the fireplace is a gorgeous abstract painting of who knows what. It's probably done by one of those whacked out hippies. His bed looks like heaven. I have a rock hard, piece of shit mattress, but his looks like a cloud. I don't even want to see his fucking bathroom. If his bedroom is any indication, his bathroom is likely modeled after a spa or some shit. Damn.

"Your room is impressive. Maybe you should get your money back from that chick and just decorate the place yourself." I laugh, but he doesn't. Ah shit, don't get all serious on me.

His fingers tighten around mine and he pulls me towards him. He turns away from me and leads the way back downstairs. He walks us into the kitchen and I'm not shocked to see that the damn thing matches the cold theme. It's all slick granite countertops and dark wood cabinetry. Each cabinet has an opaque glass center and a thin, brushed nickel handle. The appliances are all top of the line and cost more than I make in 6 months, I bet. It should be fun cooking in this kitchen. It's better than my electric hotplate, toaster oven, and microwave.

"So, is it okay if I just get to it?"

He lets my hand go and rounds the center island to sit atop a stool on the opposite side, settling down and staring at me with seemingly rapt attention.

"Have at it," he says with another panty-incinerating smile.

It smacks me square on and I swear for just a second I feel those butterflies. Butterflies? What is this shit? That's a no-go zone. I don't do the emotionally attached thing. It's never been a good idea for me. I have only ever loved three, Maman, Papa, and my job. I've already lost two of the three and the third is a hair's breadth from being ripped from me. I shoo away those thoughts; I can't deal with that right now. That shit is the whole reason I'm seeking out a night of hot sex and distraction. I start digging through his cabinets and drawers. All my depressing thoughts are soon on their way out as I throw together one of my signature dishes in Damon's sterile kitchen.

Chapter Four

Dirty Mouth

"This is the best thing I've had in ages. Really, really good, Jo. Thank you." Damon caps off his sentence by shoveling in the last heaping forkful of my famous cheeseburger casserole.

It's one of my favorite dishes to make since it's pretty cheap and easy. I make it for just myself all the time. I have never really cooked for anyone else; this is a first for me and I'm kind of enjoying the compliments. It's out of character for me to even give a shit. There's just something so damned familiar about him; something familiar and comforting. I feel like I want to be around him. Like maybe being around him will make things all right; like it will make me all right. It's fucking preposterous. I know that, but it's a feeling that I can't shake. I take another long gulp of my water and he follows suit.

"You're welcome. I've never cooked for anyone, so this is a first. Glad I didn't screw it up." I smile. What the fuck? Who cares if I screw it up? This is a one night stand, plain and simple.

"Do you want to have coffee in the library?"

"Sure."

He quickly sets the coffee maker and loads our dirty dishes into the dishwasher. I watch and wait. He looks so handsome. Those luminescent amber eyes have a way of cutting right through me and making me feel naked in the most incredible way. I've been itching to run my fingers through his dark, disheveled hair since I first laid eyes on him. He pours our coffee and makes mine just the way I like it with cream and one sugar. He must've remembered from this morning.

"Coffee. Cream and sugar."

I take the cup. "Thank you."

He offers his arm and motions for me to hook mine with his. My arm slips into the crook of his elbow and we climb the stairs arm in arm. We enter his loft library and I set down my coffee to admire the space again. I love it in here. Damn, I would kill to have a private library like this. I don't usually kid myself with having wild dreams of being highly successful. I am quite the realist, but I can't help but wish that someday I might end up lounging in a library of my own just like this one.

"I really love your library. I didn't picture you as a book lover." I glance over to him. Damn, he looks good enough to eat.

"Why?"

"Oh, I don't know. I shouldn't stereotype, but you don't look much like a man who sits around and reads."

"I don't. I never have enough time, but that's not what I mean. I mean, why do you love my library?"

What? Is he fucking dense? I work in a bookstore, for crying out loud. That should be a big indication that I have a thing for books. I furrow my brow. "I work in a bookstore. I don't imagine I'd work there if I didn't enjoy it." He arches a skeptical eyebrow and I can tell he wants to know more.

"Yes, but why do you want to work in a bookstore?"

I help myself to one of the ultra cushy chairs and take in a deep breath. He sits in the chair across from me and props his feet on the coffee table between us. Against my better judgment, I decide to toss it out there. I have nothing to lose really. Though this guy is undeniably a catch, it doesn't change my bottom line. This is a one night stand, and I don't do relationships. It wouldn't matter if I did date because I am nearly one hundred percent positive that he doesn't do relationships either. So, fuck it. I'll tell him why I have a thing for books.

"My childhood was shitty. I started living on the streets when I was twelve and I didn't have a roof over my head for six years. I used to go to the library for hours a day. It started out as a place to keep warm in the winter and cool in the summer, but then I was hooked. I didn't have anyone, but every time I walked through those doors, I felt like each author was part of my family and the characters they created were all my friends. I counted on them. None of them ever let me down or left me. They never yelled at me or hit me. They never did anything but occupy time and keep me company. They were all I ever had. All I still have. Now that the store may go out of business, it's like I'm losing my family and friends. I love all my books. Being a book lover saved my life. I spent more time reading in the library than I did putting myself at risk in the streets. I was able to teach myself what I needed to pass my GED exam. The librarian, Evelyn, never turned me away. She could have and she should have. Homeless people are not usually welcome to squat in the public library for so long, but I think she knew I wasn't just using the place for shelter. One day, she came to me with a registration card for the GED and told me to go take it. All I had to do was show up, it was all paid for. She also let me use her personal address on the paperwork, since I didn't have one. I owe a lot to her and to every book I've ever cracked open. That's why I love them, and why I work at a bookstore." I sure as hell hope he remembers what I said about apologies and how I despise them or I'm going to regret opening my mouth about my screwed up childhood.

"You have a dirty mouth, don't you," he says in a manner saturated with innuendo.

Hell yes, I have a dirty mouth. I'll show him just how dirty it is if we can cut to the chase and get rid of some clothes. I haven't gotten laid in weeks and I'm getting impatient. I stand from my chair and skirt the edge of the coffee table to get to where he is seated.

"I don't really feel like coffee and conversation anymore."

He stands and his body is so close to mine I can feel his warmth radiating outward. He leans in and his full lips brush against the rim of my ear. "Then what would you like to have, Jo?" His warm breath lights my skin on fire and my core turns to molten hot, liquid arousal.

Fuck, I want him between my thighs. "What would you like?" I whisper.

"Would you like me to show you what I want?"

"Yes."

One of his hands snakes around my waist and he

jerks me to him. My body crashes against his with such force that the air in my lungs is gone in an instant. His other hand slowly makes its way up my spine, past the nape of my neck to my hair. His fingers tangle in my wavy brown locks and he pulls my head back just enough, giving him unlimited access to my neck. His hot mouth lands on my racing pulse and he kisses and licks at my skin. His mouth greedily works a trail up my neck to my ear. He takes the lobe of my ear into his mouth and suckles just a moment before biting down lightly, coaxing a moan from me. His breathing is heavy and so is mine. I'm panting and wanton in his grasp. My body is humming with need.

His hips are flush against my body and his erection is pressed against my stomach. It's rock hard and pulsing; I can feel his cock twitching even through the cloth separating our bodies. I'm helpless in his vice-like, dominating grip. His hand hasn't left my hair and I'm pressed to him as close as I can get without having his cock filling me. Fuck, I want to feel him in me. He keeps up his ministrations on my neck and ear, then switches sides and shows the other the same amount of attention. I am soaked for him. I can feel how slick he's made me. If he doesn't take me soon, I may beg for it, and that's not my style at all. But damnit, this man does something to me that I've never experienced before. He keeps lapping at my neck and pulling my hair. His hips make one expert roll against my body. That's it. Fuck it.

"Please."

He freezes and backs away marginally to look at me. Those warm, honey eyes are my undoing.

I place my palms against the firm wall of his chest and resort to begging. "Please," I repeat sounding more desperate than the first time.

He grabs me and pulls me to him harder than the first time and growls in my ear. "I'm going to take you now. It's going to be hard and rough. Get ready."

Another moan escapes my throat and I all but melt in his embrace. He sweeps my body up into his arms and I instinctively wrap my legs around his waist as strides swiftly and purposefully down the hall to his bedroom. He kicks the door open without regard and rushes me to his bed. He hasn't kissed me yet and my lips are eager to taste him. He has me on the side of the bed and slips his hand between my knees, I allow my thighs to spread for him invitingly. A low growl of appreciation rumbles through his chest again and damn, it turns me on.

"Damon, pl-"

"Hush. Patience."

Oh, for fuck's sake. I'm going to burst if he doesn't take me now. He moves to stand between my thighs. I glance at his erection and my mouth waters to taste him. He slowly runs the palms of his hands up my thighs as he leans down to me; his lips are so close to mine. One hand grips my upper thigh, hard as hell. It's to the point of pain, yet my core stirs deliciously; it's the biggest contradiction. His other hand slips further up my thigh to the junction between my legs. I quiver in anticipation and he observantly recognizes my submission. I've never allowed anyone to have such power over me, but I want Damon to take me; all of me. It feels good to let go right now. I have no rational explanation and at the moment, I really don't give a fuck. I can only think of him. He has dominated me, body and mind, and I don't want to do a damn thing to fight against it. This feels too good to deny. His mouth is so close and I want his lips on mine; I want to feel all of him. One finger hooks into the tiny triangle of cloth that conceals my arousal and I hear a rip of fabric at the same time his mouth takes mine. His tongue slips over my lips the very same moment his finger slides into me. Fuck. I moan as his soft, wet tongue slides against mine. A second finger slips into my channel. He has consumed my mouth so completely that I can barely breathe. His tongue delves deep. My hips undulate of their own volition and it speaks to him. He breaks our kiss and his fingers withdraw. I watch as he licks both fingers clean. Oh fuck, that's hot.

"The minute I saw you in that store, I tried to imagine how good you'd taste." He pops a finger back into his mouth and slowly withdraws it. "I wasn't even close. You taste like perfection."

"Fuck me," I whine.

"Not yet," he says as he flicks open the button and zipper of my short jean skirt. In one fell swoop, he frees me of my skirt and tattered panties. He hauls my legs up until my knees are nearly touching my chest. "Hold your legs and whatever you do, don't let go until I tell you to."

I nod in understanding. What the fuck is he going to do? I should feel slightly shy being perched so openly on the side of his bed, but I have no shame. I'm too hot for him to feel anything but turned on. He gives me a devilish half smile as he stands back for a moment and admires my position. I still don't feel embarrassed, I feel aroused; very, very aroused. Before I can draw in my next breath, he bends at the waist and his hands grip my hips, his mouth landing on my drenched center. Damn. He groans and the low pitch of his voice vibrates through his chest, past his lips, and right against my needy flesh.

I whimper and writhe beneath his mouth. His grip on my hips tightens painfully, yet again, my core stirs deliciously. It's fucking baffling. His lips kiss me, then I feel his tongue dart into me. He licks and laps at me. Fast, then slow. Deep strokes of his tongue against my inner walls and short, shallow flicks at my opening build me to climax in no time. I feel like I'm on the edge of bliss. He plunges two fingers back inside me as his attention hones in on my clit. His mouth covers the tight bunch of pulsing nerves and I moan loudly. The grip on my legs slips and they drop a fraction. His mouth leaves my clit and his fingers withdraw.

"Oh fuck, please don't stop," I plead. I glance at him as I pant and work at catching my breath. He draws the zipper of his jeans down and hooks his thumbs into the waistband of his underwear and frees his erection. He kicks away his jeans and underwear. Holy shit! His cock is perfect. It's thick and long and everything I could want. His skin is pink and looks soft. I want to touch his rigid, pulsing length. I want to slip it into my mouth and taste him.

"I told you not to let go of your legs, didn't I?"

What? Is he seriously going to yell at me for getting lost in the moment? Before I can say a damn thing, he wrenches me up from the bed and whirls me around. He pulls my shirt over my head and hooks his finger into my bra strap. He pulls back the elastic and then releases it. The strap pops against my skin and I jump, mostly out of surprise. He leans into me and his erection presses against my backside.

"I told you not to let go."

"I know."

"I told you this would be rough. Are you ready?"

"Fuck, yes."

"You have a filthy mouth."

I glance back just in time to see him finish rolling a condom down the length of his erection.

"Get ready, Jo."

A moment of worry comes over me. What if he hurts me? What if he is some weirdo freak who does strange shit in the bedroom? I'm okay with rough sex, but if things get weird, I don't know if I can fight him off. He leans over and brushes his lips against the rim of my ear again. It sends chills skating over my body and all worrisome thoughts disappear.

"You're safe with me," he coos.

I believe him and it's absurd. I have nothing to base that off of. I don't know why, but damn it, I do feel safe with him. I can't explain it. All I know is that he feels exquisite and I trust him with my body. I nod and his fingers go back to my opening from behind. He smoothes my arousal over me.

"So wet." He nudges the wide tip of his cock against me and I inch my legs even further apart for him. The head of his erection slips like silk over my flesh and he pauses, poised with just the tip inside me. "Tell me what you want," he demands and I don't hesitate.

"I want you. I want your cock," I whine.

"Tell me you're ready for me."

"Please, I'm ready for you." My voice is so breathy I hardly recognize it.

He eases into me a little more, then withdraws to just the tip again. I whimper, desperate for more. Suddenly, he slams into me and sheaths his entire thick, pulsing length within my greedy body. His cock knocks the wind out of me and I gasp to regain my breath. I can feel the tip of his erection bump against the depths of my insides. It's a feeling I've never experienced before and the thought of him being the first to fill me so completely is exhilarating. He rears back and hauls right back into me with astounding power. He pulls out and plows through me again. Each deep thrust knocks the wind from me and I struggle to take even short choppy breaths. One of his hands slips around my side and he presses his palm low on my abdomen, his other hand against the small of my back. He holds me immobile in this position while he drives into me over and over. With his hand pressing against my stomach, I can feel the tip of his cock butting against the center of me even more. It's a strong sensation of pleasure and pain.

"You like it, don't you?" he grunts into my ear.

Hell yes, I like it. I fucking love it. He's the best lover I have ever had, hands down. Without warning, he freezes in place and the hand on the small of my back disappears only to reappear with a hard smack across my bare, perched up ass.

I gasp. "Oh fuck, that's hot."

"Tell me," he demands.

I comply instantly. I would do anything right about now just to get him to move in me again. "I love it," I blurt.

His warm palm sweeps over my reddened ass and my insides stir with renewed desire. On a groan, he buries himself inside me once more. I shiver as he starts to move again. His thrusts become harder and even faster than before. My feet are no longer on the ground; my legs are spread wide. My knees are bent so that my feet go skyward. He grips his hands hard on my hipbones and pulls me to him as he thrusts forward. I feel weightless like this. I fist my hands into his bedding as my stomach clenches down deep. Electricity begins coursing from the tips of my fingers and toes, through arms and legs to meet in a violent climactic crash in my center. My body grabs at his erection. I gasp and shudder. Every muscle tightens and pleasure consumes me completely. My eyes roll back and he crashes into me once more, then groans and grunts as his own release takes him over the edge.

"Damon!" I scream with what little breath and energy is left in me. All else has been exhausted. My body quivers and quakes in his grips. He stays planted within me as he leans forward to rest his chest against my back. I can feel the mist of sweat across his skin and the pounding of his heart as I come down from my blissful orgasm. I'm so spent, I feel unable to move an inch. Now is usually the point where I gather my clothes and say "see you never again,"" but I can't seem to speak. Maybe he'll say it.

He stays where he is for a few more moments while we both catch our breath and slow our hearts. He finally pulls out of me and turns me to face him. His erection hasn't gone anywhere; damn my horny self for wanting more of him.

I open my mouth to speak, but he puts his big hand over my lips before I can form my lame ass, awkward post hook up speech.

He shakes his head side to side. "No. This isn't what you're thinking."

So awkward. He walks into what looks like his bathroom and reappears a moment later. We stand before each other, completely naked. This is the worst part about one time hook ups. There's always the awkward post-sex chat. It sometimes makes me want to quit doing this and just give relationships a shot. The idea of it scares the shit out of me, but this hooking up thing is getting old. Not to mention the fact that I've never been *this* lucky before. Damon is the best I've ever had. The idea of sleeping with someone with less sexual prowess than Damon depresses me even further.

"Listen, I get it. It's no big deal. I'm not the type of woman who equates sex with a relationship. This was a one-time thing," I move to recover my clothing and his arms scoop me off my feet and he body slams me to his mattress. I bounce high off the plush bedding and he is quick to cover my body with his.

"No, that's just my point. This is not what you say it is. You say this is a one-time thing. I say it isn't."

Whoa. What? "Um, tap your breaks, boss. What are you talking about?"

He chuckles and it's infectious. I kind of want to laugh with him.

"That dirty mouth of yours is kind of cute, too." He leans forward and presses his lips to mine and they feel amazing. We drink from each other greedily for a long moment. The kiss ends and we're both panting and hungry to have each other again. Damn.

"If this isn't what I think it is, then tell what you

think it is."

He shifts his legs so that one knee comes between mine and nudges them apart. My legs fall away from each other in compliance. He settles his hips between my thighs and his solid erection pulses against my stomach. He wrenches my arms above my head and easily pins them both with one big hand. The other hand grasps my jaw, forcing me to look him in the face.

"When I met you this morning, something strange happened and I don't know what it is yet. Until I find out what it was, this is not over. I want you. You want me. I plan on having you as much as I can."

Just who the hell is he? I'll admit, the dominant thing is hot in bed, but I'm the only one in charge of my life. I never waver on that. "And what if I say hell no, absolutely not?"

"You won't. You felt it too, I know you did. I saw it in those green eyes of yours."

He's right. I want more of him. How the hell could I refuse this kind of sex? No woman on the face of the planet would refuse him. I can agree to this. It's not like I'm agreeing to marry him; I'm agreeing to more sex. That's all. No big deal. "Okay, fine. Sex. I can stand a little more sex with you."

"Fine." He smiles wide, baring his pearly whites,

and releases my wrists, running one hand down my side at a painfully slow, seductive pace. His lips press against my neck and he begins to kiss a hot, wet trail down to my chest. He grips my hip in one hand while the other goes to my breasts and massages my flesh. He takes a nipple into his mouth and I moan.

"Your bed is nice," I murmur.

"Is it?" he says with a mouth full of my breast, sucking hard before releasing my taut nipple.

"Yep. Much nicer than my crappy bed."

"If you think my bed is nice, you should see my bathtub." In one graceful movement, he sweeps me out of the bed and sets me to my feet. I sway slightly and grab onto his muscular arm. He holds me by the shoulders until my spotty vision clears.

"Got up too fast."

"Sorry. Better now?"

"Better," I affirm.

Chapter Five

Jogging

Damon drags me to his crazy-big, modern bathroom and I stand and wait while he turns on the taps to fill the mammoth tub. His muscles ripple and flex as he moves and I drink it in. The sight of this gorgeous man in the nude is a real treat. I have to admit that I'm a bit excited to prolong this hook up. He leans over the tub and pours in some girly bath shit. I'm sure he assumes I like that crap and use it often. He would be wrong; I don't use bath stuff because I don't take baths. I don't even have a tub. So even if I wanted to, I couldn't. My shitty apartment came with a tiny stall shower and that's it. I'd move out of the place, but the rent is cheap and I've been there for seven years. I can't really afford moving expenses anyway and I especially won't be moving now that the store is in trouble.

My serious thoughts have distracted me from Damon. He steps behind me and pulls me back into his chest. I glance at our reflection in the mirror and panic, sheer panic, courses through me. We look good together; we look like a couple. His amber eyes contrast against my green in a way that has me staring in spite of my nerves. His nearly black, disheveled hair looks even darker and shinier against my medium brown waves. His skin is darker than mine. Working in a bookstore all day doesn't allow for much sun bathing. I stand frozen in his arms. I am naked and freaked out, but fascinated at the same time. He grasps my jaw and keeps me looking forward at the mirror.

"See? You felt it, too, and now you see it," he whispers in my ear and I know he's right.

When he touched me this morning, something familiar flashed in my brain and now, seeing our reflection, it feels like déjà vu, but I can't figure this shit out. This is so not my thing; I'm driving blind here. I'm about to take a bath with a man I met less than twenty-four hours ago. We just met this morning, but I can't seem to shake the feeling that I've seen him before. It's going to drive me nuts until I figure out how I know him. I say nothing and stare blankly until he releases me to turn off the water. He sweeps my hand up in his and tugs me toward the tub.

"Get in." He holds my hand and I step into the huge tub and sink down into the soothing water. His tall, dark, handsome body sinks down and the water level rises significantly. He reaches forward and easily hauls me across the tub to where he is leaned back, wedging me between his muscular thighs.

I'm completely lost in thought, dreamily enjoying the bath and him.

"Tell me what you're thinking, Jo."

Fuck it. "Fine. I'm thinking that this is weird."

He brushes my hair over my shoulder, cups water in his hands and pours it down my back. "Elaborate?"

"I'll admit the whole familiarity thing. But I don't do...this." I raise a hand in the air and whirl it in a circle.

"I don't either," he admits.

"Then why the hell bother with me? Neither one of us does relationships. Quite frankly, I've never dated, like, ever."

"You've never had a boyfriend?"

"Not many guys pining for homeless chicks," I say sarcastically and shrug. "Besides, I just don't want to build a relationship with someone. It always ends one way or another and it's never pretty. So why bother?"

"I get your logic, but I'm not asking you to commit

J.L. Mac

to a relationship with me." He keeps at his water pouring duties as we try to sort out what the hell is going on between us.

"You're not?" Now I feel dumb.

"No. I get it. But I can't *not* figure out what this is...between us. It'll kill me if I don't."

"I know, it's weird."

"All right, let's make a deal."

My hands stroke small circles across the tops of his thighs as he talks.

"Let's just agree to see each other until we can sort out why the hell it seems like we've already met. You'll see me every day. We spend as much time together as we can until it comes to one of us. No strings attached. Just great sex and jogging memories. Deal?"

I think I can manage that. It feels a lot better than I thought it would. It sounds fine, actually. I like him. He's nice, brilliant in bed, as handsome as they come, and apparently we know each other. Screw it. This can be fun. "Okay. You demonstrated the great sex part already. How do you plan on jogging our memories? My memory is pretty damn spot on, so what if this is just our imagination at work here?"

I turn to face him and he accommodates my shifting position, pulling me to him. He scoots to the center of the tub and I wrap my legs around his waist.

"That's easy, but very juvenile. Twenty questions. Let's play."

I laugh and wrap my arms around his neck to stroke his hair. "Fine, I guess."

"I'll go first. Where have you worked?"

"That's easy, since the bookstore is the only job I've ever had. Now my turn; how old are you?"

"I think I may be a little older than you." He looks at me sheepishly and I melt. He can't be much older than me. I raise a prompting eyebrow.

"I'm thirty-three. How old are you?"

"I'm twenty-five." I shrug. "Have you ever been one of those volunteers at the mission down on Tenth?"

He looks at me incredulously. "No. Maybe I've met you at one of the clubs?"

"Don't hang out in clubs. I don't exactly have any friends to go to clubs or bars with. What do you do for a living?"

"I own and invest. I have multiple clubs here in Vegas. I also own three five-star restaurants and invest in various business ventures."

"Oh, I see. You're a suit," I say tauntingly, only because he's definitely not a boring suit.

"Big time suit. Family?"

Please don't go there. I take in a deep breath and let it all out. "I have no siblings and my parents are dead, hence the whole homeless thing. You?"

He nods and looks to the wall behind me. He's quiet for a moment and I wait while I run my fingers in figure eights on the back of his neck. "I don't speak to my dad and I never knew my real mother."

Damn. I never could have predicted that one. He seems pretty put together. I mean, anyone can look at me and tell that I'm screwed up. I swear way too much and have no desire to correct my ugly habit. I smoke when I drink. I let my dirty dishes stack up before I wash them. I wear my jeans a few times before I wash them and I've spent far longer than a few days in the same clothes before. I find the idea of love and family and all that jazz a waste. The point is, I have some screwed up philosophies and habits. Damon has no telltale signs of being fucked up, so maybe he isn't.

"Let's get out, the water's getting cold."

I uncoil myself from around him and grip the side of the tub to get out. "Oh fuck! Shit, shit, shit," I cry as I realize the mistake I have made.

"What's wrong?!"

I want to cry. I'm so dumb. I got into the tub with my mother's watch on and the second hand has stopped ticking. I don't cry often, but tears pool in my eyes and my chin quivers.

"Jo, what's wrong?" Damon's voice is stern and it snaps me out of my pitiful daze.

I look at him with tears streaming down my face. Fuck, I won't forgive myself for this. It's all I have of Maman's. She was so proud of it. Papa gave her this watch for their first anniversary. She told me he worked a second job for months to save for it. She wore it with pride and he knew his hard work was worth it. Now it doesn't work and I don't know if it can be fixed. Even if it *can* be fixed, I can't afford to pay for repairs right now. "My watch," I say weakly through my tears.

He reaches out and takes my wrist in his. He examines the watch for a moment and I know it must be broken because his face goes blank. Fuck my life. He releases the delicate clasp and examines the watch closer, flipping it over. Sometimes I forget about the inscription on the underside of the watch. It says, *"Collette, mon cœur réside avec vous pour toujours plus."* It's in French, and even though my French is rusty, I can still read it and speak it decently. Damon looks at me and pity fills his eyes. I know the look. I hate that look but somehow, coming from him, it doesn't quite feel like pity. It feels like understanding and I let it go. My mother's ruined watch is my only concern at the moment.

"What does it say?" he asks on a whisper.

"Collette, my heart resides with you forevermore," I translate weakly, tears continuing to slip down my cheeks.

He nods and looks to me. "What did you say your last name was again? I'll have this fixed. They'll need to know the name of the owner."

"Geroux. My full name is Josephine Lisette Geroux."

"I'm going to make this right. I promise you, Josephine."

I don't bother correcting him about my name. I am completely entranced by the sincerity and emotion written across his features. He enfolds me in a plush towel and slings one around his waist, leading me back to his bedroom. I glance at the clock on his nightstand; it reads 12:26am. How in the hell have I been with him for over six hours already? He peels back the comforter on his sinfully comfortable bed and says nothing as he lifts me beneath the arms to place me on the mattress. I don't protest; I have no fight tonight. I'm beaten down from the day I've endured. Damon slips into the bed beside me and tugs me to him. I lay my head on his shoulder and cry, allowing myself a measure of self-pity for my shitty day. Sixteen years have passed since my world caved in. I have fought and been strong every day since then. That's exactly five-thousand-eight-hundred and forty days of fighting and being strong. I know because I have counted the days since the accident. It's another habit I can't kick. So, today, day 5,840, I will feel sorry for myself and let Damon feel sorry for me too.

"I'm going to make it better."

I sniffle and swipe the tears from my cheeks. "I promise I am not a big whine bag. It's just...it's all I have left."

"What do you mean?"

"They've been gone for sixteen years today. My mom's watch is all I have of them and I ruined it like an adolescent idiot. I knew it wasn't waterproof. My mom always took it off when she did the dishes. I remember that."

Damon rolls me to my back and scoots down the bed to kneel between my legs. I lay naked before him in tears and he doesn't seem bothered. He picks up one foot and kisses my instep. I shiver as a zap of electricity races through me. He kisses my ankle and another zap races through my nerve endings. He begins dropping a trail of tender kisses up my legs. He stops at the scar on my shin.

"How did you get this?" he asks as he stares at the ugly reminder of the accident.

"I have the asshole that killed my parents to thank for that. I was in the backseat when we were hit head on. I had a compound fracture."

He inhales deeply and looks at me. Anger flashes in his eyes for a moment and it seems so out of place. He has no reason to be angry. I'm the one with the fucked up scar and the dead parents. He raises my leg and presses his lips to my scar, then rests his forehead against the ugly reminder.

"I know you don't want to hear it, but I have to say it. I'm sorry. I'm so sorry."

His sincere apology causes a new round of tears to fill and spill. He comes back to my side and envelopes me in his solid arms. I lie naked in his arms, physically and emotionally spent. I don't give him shit about the apology. I can't. His words were the definition of genuine and I can't be upset with him for it. "I should probably go home soon."

"No. Stay with me tonight."

"I've never sta-"

"Doesn't matter. Stay with me."

"Okay." I feel his chest deflate and I'm positive that he's content with my answer. My tears fade away and I drift off to sleep in Damon's bed, completely unsure of what the fuck I have gotten myself into.

Chapter Six

Mirage

It's so loud. My ears ring and the background noises are muffled. Damn, I ache all over. I hear sirens. Wait. Sirens? What happened? Fuck. My heart beats wildly in my chest and my breathing is erratic. I'm panicking and I have no idea what's going on. I need to check my body. I look down and see blood. It's everywhere; it's all over me. My hands are stained crimson and I run my hands over my body to see where I am wounded, but nothing. I'm not hurt. It's not my blood. I look around, but everything is blurry. Where am I? I rub my eyes and my vision clears enough to see two figures in the distance. Maman and Papa. It's them! Maman! Papa! I scream for them, but I don't think they hear me because they haven't stopped. Maman! Papa! Please! Don't leave me again! Please! Don't go! They won't stop. They keep walking away and I'm reduced to nothing. I fall to my knees and plead. "Don't leave me. Don't leave me. Don't leave me. Please stay. Come back!" My shoulders slump forward in defeat as I watch their figures disappear in the distance, a taunting mirage. I lurch back and forth with painfully intense sobs that rip through me, leaving a quaking, wounded soul in its wake.

"Come back to me," says a voice in the distance. "Please. Please. Please." I startle and jolt awake when I feel strong arms tangle around me.

"Fuck, Jo! You scared the shit out of me. Shhh... You had a nightmare, you're okay now. It's not real."

I shake in his embrace and work on calming my breathing and pulse. He has no clue just how real my dream was. I wish I could agree with him and say that it's not real, but it is. My parents are still dead and I'm as alone as a person can be. I have no family or friends. Only Sutton's old ass and now Damon, and I'm not even sure what the hell I agreed to with him.

He turns me to face him and wipes sweat from my brow with his thumb. "Want to talk about it?"

"No."

"You're okay, Jo. Go back to sleep." He turns me back to my other side and pulls my back to his chest again. He tucks me under his arm protectively and it's a magical cure. In this position, with him, I feel safe. My eyelids are heavy and I give into slumber.

I wake up to my phone chiming. "Shut up." I groan and cover my head with my pillow. The phone silences and begins ringing all over again. I leap from the bed and instantly remember where I am. The luxurious carpet beneath my bare feet is my first reminder. Shit, I'm naked. I snatch up my annoying cell phone first. "Hello?" I snap down the line.

"Jo, I need you in early today. I have some things I need you to get done right away," Sutton barks.

"What could you possibly need done right away?"

"We're liquidating. It's over."

"No! You can't give up yet. We can figure it out!"

"I can't afford it. We have to crate up inventory and start selling it off. Store's done. I'll see you shortly." Sutton hangs up on me before I can form a rebuttal.

I crawl back into the empty bed and cradle my head in my hands. Where is Damon? No, stop; I can't think about Damon right now, I have bigger issues. Fuck. This is really happening. It's over; the store is really going to close. What am I going to do? Nobody's hiring right now. I'd be lucky to get a job flipping burgers or cleaning toilets. There's another bookstore close to my place, but it's a giant chain store and they'd never hire me. I don't kiss ass, make coffee, or act bubbly like some cheerleader. I damn sure don't believe in that "the customer is always right" bullshit. That's a steaming pile of horse shit and I refuse to deal with it. If some jerk off wants to argue with me about something that I know he's wrong about, I am going to tell him. If some lady's kid is clowning in the store and knocks something over and causes damage, guess what? Mommy of the Year is going to pay for it. I get that it's good business etiquette to kiss ass when necessary, but I just can't. It isn't in me. No one will hire someone like me. I'm too rough around the edges. I don't have a college education; I have a lousy GED and that's it. I'm royally screwed.

"What's wrong?"

I snap out of my thoughts at the sound of Damon's voice and zero in on him, standing bare-chested in the doorway of the bedroom, staring at me. I grab the sheet and quickly wrap it around myself. "I have to go. My boss called, he needs me in early. I guess we're liquidating inventory. The store is closing." I scan the room for my clothes and spot them on the floor.

Damon remains in the doorway, his black pajama pants drawing my eyes to all the right places; his bare chest, the trail of hair on his abdomen, and his beautiful, sloppy mess of dark hair are all begging for my touch. He looks perfect and the memory of that amazing cock buried within me sends a shiver down my spine. He walks towards me and climbs onto the bed, pulls me down to my back and wraps his arms around me, hauling me to his chest. I think he likes me in this position. I huff in exasperation. I really don't have time for this cuddling bullshit. Sutton needs my help ending the only good thing in my life. Wonderful. Just fucking grand. I hate this. I can't stand the idea of it being sold and turned into some cookie cutter yogurt shop or tanning salon.

"Tell me about it."

"I can't. I have to get over there."

"Tell me."

"Damnit, fine. We've been struggling for some time, so I knew it was coming; I was just holding out a little hope that things would turn around, you know? I have some great ideas that might help our profit margin, or lack thereof. Well, anyway, Sutton has to sell the inventory and close down. He can't afford to stay in business any longer." Tears sting the backs of my eyes and the lump in my throat builds. What the hell is wrong with me? I never cry this much. I glance at Damon and he appears to be digesting what I've said.

"So you're unemployed now?"

"Gee thanks, asshole. Don't lessen the blow on my

account."

He chuckles and nods. "Okay, you're right, that was rude. It's the business part of me. Don't worry about it, Josephine. It will all work out."

"Hmph!" He would say that shit to me right now. It's just like all those damn volunteers used to say, "Don't worry. Things are going to work out." I don't need or want to be fed a line of bullshit. It doesn't make me feel any better and it damn sure doesn't change the bottom line. It only pisses me off. Things never just work out on their own! If things work out for me, it will be because I did what I had to do to change my life. That's the bottom line. There is no genie in a lamp, no lucky penny found, and no magical wishing well. All that shit is a fairytale that I don't buy into. The store closing is a problem, but I'll just have to find a way to manage. I've done it before and I'll do it again. I'll be okay. I peel myself from his arms and dress, minus one pair of destroyed panties. "I really have to get to the store."

Damon looks less than happy about me leaving. That's the last thing I need right now. "Promise you'll call me once you get out of there."

So he's a bossy ass in and out of bed, but, I have to admit that it's hot. There's something sexy about his commanding style, maybe because it's new to me. That's it.

I like it because this is my first experience with a man like him. I don't feel so uncomfortable with my strange feelings toward him now, it's new and exciting is all. I'll get over it in a day or two and his bossy attitude will be annoying and short lived. This works. I'll play along with him, for now. "I would call, but I don't think I have your number."

A sly grin spreads across his soft lips and it spells out mischief. I grab my cell phone and scroll through my extremely short list of contacts and there he is. He's the only "D" in my list of contacts. He has given me his cell number, office number and email. Wow. I nod my head up and down as I observe the new info my phone. "Okay, I guess I do have your number." I glance at him and half smile. "I'll call you when I'm free."

"Howard has your keys at the security desk."

I'm dressed and prepared to endure my walk of shame when I feel his arm hook around my waist and pull me to him. He turns me by my shoulders to face him.

"Call me," he murmurs.

His lips press against mine and my knees instantly go weak for him. Oh, these lips feel incredible pressed to mine. I will definitely want more of Damon. I don't feel so skeptical about agreeing to see him anymore; I'm really digging what he does to me. I can't walk away after just one night. Not just yet.

Chapter Seven

Captain

I smile the familiar dinging of the old silver bell signaling my entrance into the bookstore. I take three steps in and see nothing but packing crates and tissue paper. The sight of it all drives it home that we're closing; it makes me angry with everything. "Son-of-a-bitch!" I spin on my heels, sweep three fat hardbacks from the closest shelf, and stack them on the floor in front of the door. I stomp up on them and snatch the still-dinging bell down with all the force I can muster. The thin leather strap it hangs from snaps and I dust off the bell before shoving it into my bag. I'm pissed. Sutton may have the power to close up shop, but damnit, I am keeping this fucking bell!

"I called you an hour and a half ago. ASAP means as soon as possible. Where have you been?"

"Thank you for clearing that up for me, Captain Obvious. I was banging this guy I may or may not know," I answer honestly in the most flat, indifferent tone I can conjure up. Fucking nosey-ass Sutton really knows how to pluck each and every one of my nerves.

He scoffs and navigates his thin frame between two tall stacks of boxes. "I have a buyer for about two-thirds of our inventory, so we need it boxed, labeled and ready for delivery by the end of today."

"Great," I draw out, feigning excitement.

He's undoubtedly going to go lounge in his office where he'll likely snooze for most of the day while I bust my ass to get these gargantuan piles of books packed up. The bastard could at the very least get the labels done while I do the lifting and packing. But, that's Sutton for you; grumpy, lazy, asshole. We tolerate each other, but most days he makes me feel like some pesky annoyance and I do my best to make him feel ancient. We're two birds of a feather really, and we work well together. Truth is, I guess I'm just as pissy and grumpy as he is. It must be why he won't hire anyone else, not that anyone could work for him. If he hired help for me, they would quit the first day. Once they got a dose of both of us, the poor sucker would hightail it to the nearest therapist. I can be just as rough as Sutton, I guess, and I don't even realize when I'm doing it. Sutton will come to me occasionally and remind me what a raging bitch I was to a customer. Honest to God, I don't mean to be rude. It's a natural kind of royal bitchiness, I suppose, and sometimes I do feel bad about it. I try to tone it down, but I'm just one of those generally unhappy people. If you're looking for lollipops and rainbows while you shop for the latest best seller, you'd best not come to me; I won't chat you up or tell you how cute your kid is; I won't smile and flirt; I won't stroke your ego and compliment the jewelry you're wearing or the shirt you have on. I will, however, help you find what you need. I'll recommend books and hell, I'll even talk about what I liked about one book over another, but all that other shit is just not my thing.

I remember when I waltzed into the store to ask for a job. Sutton's shiny, bald head was barely visible from behind the counter and I waited for him to get up. He popped up from behind the counter and damn near had a fucking stroke. I guess he probably thought I was going to rob him or something. I looked like your typical homeless kid, even though I did my best to clean up before I came to the store. The jeans I had on were far too big, and seriously dirty. They hung off of me so I had this bungee cord that I fashioned into a belt. It was embarrassing, but losing my pants would have been worse. I remember wearing a white shirt I found on a bench beside some basketball courts. It smelled like a sweaty man, so I washed it in the water fountain at the park. My hair was rarely clean back, then so it stayed tied back. I was a top notch bum, "cleaned up" and looking for a job.

"Geez, cool it, chief. I'm not going to bite."

Sutton's brows rocketed up at mach speed. I guess I surprised him with my mouth. It happened a lot.

"And who the hell are you?"

"Miss USA, and you?"

"Captain America. Can I help you?"

I couldn't help it and giggled under my breath. "Fitting name. I want a job," I stated, very matter of fact.

He crossed his arms over his chest and looked at me like I had sprouted a second head right in front of his eyes. "And why in hell would I hire a bum?"

"I can tell you why. I love books. Probably more than you do. I have likely read every book in this store. I can tell you authors' names, along with their works, off the top of my head. I live in a book most days and dream of them most nights. I'm honest. I know how to work my ass off and I won't bail on you. Clearly, I'm in no position to throw away a steady job. Not hiring me would be a loss on your part, *Captain.*"

"Favorite author?"

"J.D. Salinger."

"*Catcher in the Rye*, huh?"

"You got it."

"Fine. You're hired, but you have to clean yourself up more. I'll expect you to look presentable. I don't want to smell you and neither do the customers. My granddaughter left for college and some of her old clothes are in my attic. I can bring you some decent pants and shirts. Just this once, though. Once you get your first paycheck, I'll expect you to buy your own clothes, girl."

"Jo. My name is Jo. Call me that or nothing at all."

"Fine. I'm Mr. Sutton. See you tomorrow morning, Jo. Don't be late or I'll fire you."

"I'll be here, Captain."

I snap out of my reminiscing when my phone buzzes against my butt cheek. I stand and pull it from my pocket. I have a text from Mr. Tall, Dark and Handsome.

Can I steal you away for lunch? Subs?

I sigh. I honestly would love to see Damon right now. I could use the distraction from this disaster, but I can't go. I have entirely too much to do around here. I plan on conning Sutton into ordering takeout for us. He'll do it; he always does. I send a text back.

Sounds great but I can't. Swamped here.

I hate that I have to spend my lunch with Sutton instead of Damon. I'm teetering on the edge of a total nuclear meltdown today. I'm dealing with the after effects of the sixteenth anniversary of the accident, I had an awful nightmare reliving all those feelings of abandonment, and I agreed to...whatever with Damon. I feel completely unlike myself and it's fucking with my head. I could use a glass of wine or two. I stride over to Sutton's office and walk right in. The old grump is knocked out cold in his old chair.

"Sutton!"

The old man lurches up out of his seat, looking like he's going to have a coronary and I end up feeling just a tad guilty for startling him.

"God-bless-it, Jo! You scared the shit out of me."

"You wear those old man diapers, so you'll be okay. Are you going to order some lunch for your slave girl or shall I starve while you dash my hopes and dreams?"

"Oh, cut the shit, Jo. You know this is hard on me, too. What the hell do you want to eat?"

"We can order Chinese from that place you like."

"Gives me heartburn."

"Everything gives you heartburn," I toss over my shoulder as I walk out of his office to get the menu from under the front counter.

"Holy hell!" I nearly jump out of my skin at the sight of Damon in front of the counter holding a big, brown paper sack. "You scared the shit out of me!"

"Sorry. I didn't mean to scare you. You said you were swamped, so I thought you'd like some lunch?" He grins, very proud of his charming gesture, no doubt.

I smile and snatch the bag from him. "What the hell did you bring? This thing is heavy!"

He shrugs and looks sheepish again, which does something weird to my insides. I get all mushy when he looks at me with those bashful amber eyes.

"I don't really know what you like yet, so I bought one of each."

There are enough sub sandwiches in the bag to feed a dozen people. I can't believe he would order all this food. I would've eaten whatever he brought. The gesture alone has me feeling gushy and giddy. It's bizarre.

"Oh, and I didn't know what you wanted to drink, so I got a variety."

"Thank you." My smile broadens and I swear, it feels like the first time I have smiled...ever.

"You're breathtaking, you know that?" His voice is low and lust filled. It makes my insides stir and crave his touch.

I set both bags on the counter and step forward, getting up on my tiptoes to kiss him. I wrap my arms around his neck and his chiseled arms enfold me. He pulls me into him and lifts me off my feet. I lean in to cover his mouth with mine and do my best to show him my appreciation. Not just for the lunch, but for the distraction, too. I feel like my world is crumbling beneath my feet, but in walks Damon and suddenly I have something to grab onto. It's frightening and comforting at the same time. His velvet tongue slips over my lips and moves rhythmically against mine. I moan into his mouth and his arms tighten around me. I can feel his erection pressed against me and damn, I wish we were at his place right about now. I can feel my skin flush with heat and arousal. I break away from his amazing lips and press my cheek to his while I catch my breath.

"Has anything come to mind yet?"

"No." I answer honestly. I still have no clue why I feel like I know him and really haven't had much time today to explore my memories.

"You?"

"No. Nothing."

"Let's eat." He lays another kiss on my lips before setting me on my feet. I sigh and grab his hand to lead him to the back of the store, where I usually eat lunch with Sutton. I pop my head into Sutton's office; the old bastard is sleeping again. Pitiful. Maybe it's a good thing the store is closing, he really should have retired a long time ago. I don't want to give him another heart attack, but I know he is hungry.

"Pssst!" His eyes crack open and he peers at me sleepily.

I grin and hold up the bag. "Lookie, lookie, Captain. Come eat, old man."

He rumbles and grumbles under his breath as he sits up then stands, pushing away his rickety chair. One day that chair's going to give out and he's going to break a fucking hip. I've told him that, but he ignores me. We sit down at the small table at the back of the store and I drag over an extra chair for Damon, then dig out the multitude of subs and make the introductions.

"Damon, this is my boss, Stanley Sutton. Sutton, this is my friend, Damon Cole." They shake hands and Sutton eyes Damon speculatively.

"Friend, huh?" Sutton grumbles.

I give him the stink eye, but he ignores it. I'm afraid he's grown too accustomed to my dirty looks over the years. "Yep. Friends. That all right by you?"

Damon says nothing, entertained by me verbally duke it out with Sutton.

"Fine by me, as long as it doesn't interfere with your work." He stares across the small table at Damon; I can tell they're sizing each other up, exchanging subliminal man thoughts or something. I don't get it, but whatever. I've never introduced Sutton to anyone I've hooked up with for obvious reasons. I have the feeling Sutton may be a tiny bit territorial here. Maybe he's being protective?

"Okay boys, chill out. Let's eat. Sutton, you want the ham and Swiss, right?"

I don't have to ask. I have been ordering his food for seven years. I know him better than even he knows himself some days.

"Yeah," he mumbles as he pops open a soda.

I glance at Damon and he watches me observantly. I sort through the sandwiches and choose turkey on wheat for myself, Damon picks one and we all devour our food. As I begin clearing our mess and putting away the leftovers, I hear Sutton clear his throat.

"Damon, may I have a word?"

I pause and shoot a death glare in Sutton's direction. He doesn't even acknowledge my irritation.

"Of course." Damon winks at me before following Sutton into his office.

I hear the door click shut and I debate whether or not I should eavesdrop. Fuck it. I don't care. Let them talk. I finish cleaning up from lunch and busy myself with labels while I wait for Mr. Tall, Dark and Handsome to reappear. A full half an hour later, I hear the office door open and Damon walks toward me. I can't help it. I want to know what they were talking about.

"I have to get back to the office. I have some time sensitive matters that need my attention. Walk me out?"

I look for any clues of what the hell just happened in Sutton's office, but Damon gives away nothing. He's as calm and cool as he could possibly be. It leaves me feeling perplexed, to say the very least. "Sure."

He extends his hand to me and I take it. He leads us out the front door and we walk at a snail's pace to his car. This time he's driving a BMW and it matches his appearance. He looks every bit the businessman with the car and his amazing self-clad in a gray suit, dusky blue shirt, and silver tie.

"You should know that he loves you."

I snap my head back in shock. "What?"

"Sutton. He loves you. Trust me."

I scoff and shake my head. "He doesn't love me; that's total bullshit. He can barely stand me and trust me, the feeling is mutual."

He chuckles in amusement, releasing my hand and cupping my face in his big hands. My heart speeds up and my stomach flutters. He's just so damn handsome and charming. He has no glitches; he seems to be perfect, aside from his semi-screwed up childhood. He's got to be too good to be true; there's no other explanation.

"You have a dirty mouth," he breathes.

"Yeah, but I think you like my dirty mouth."

"I like a whole lot more than this mouth of yours." He runs his thumb across the seam of my lips and I bite it. He sucks in air through gritted teeth and fire blazes in those amber eyes. "Text me your address. I'm picking you up as soon as you get home from work. Your ass is *mine* tonight. All night."

His lips silence the protest that I was contemplating making. Oh, to hell with it. I kiss him back, giving as good as I got. I agreed to more sex and I'm a woman of my word. Besides, I won't deny that I'm starving for more of him. He ends the kiss too soon for my liking and I groan in protest. He smiles and presses my cheek to his stubbly jaw, wrapping me up in a tight hug.

"Okay," I say softly.

He plants a kiss on my cheek, slips into his fancy-ass car and drives away, leaving me to count the seconds until I feel his skin against mine again.

Chapter Eight

Dinner Plans

I turn and stride back to the store. When I walk in, I see Sutton busying himself with my abandoned labels. I put my hands on my hips and fire away. "What the hell was that all about?"

Sutton peeks up at me as nonchalantly as he can. "What?"

Oh, he's really pressing his luck today. "Don't you play dumb with me, Captain! Why did you drag him into your office and just what the hell did you two talk about? You put on a big display at lunch too, by the way. Nice. Very nice." Why the hell does his lack of courtesy towards Damon have me so riled? I shouldn't care, but I do. This can't be good news.

"I had to have words with him. Last I checked, this is America and I'm free to talk to whoever I please, so don't get your panties in a twist, you prima donna."

My blood boils and I see red. How dare he make fun of me. I'm no damn prima donna; I never have been and never will be. "Don't you dare talk to me like that, Captain! I'm no fucking prima donna and my panties are not in a twist!" I growl at him and his face falls a little. What the hell? Is that remorse? I didn't think he was capable of that emotion.

"I apologize, okay. I was only joking with the name calling. I just wanted to check him out. Too many jackasses out there these days; it's not safe for young women to just pick up any man." He shrugs and my jaw hits the floor. He gives a shit?

"Babysitting me, huh?"

"Well, someone has to! You're as careless as they come. Now...stop...lollygagging and get to work here. I'm uh...going to be in my office." He shoves his hands in his pockets and fidgets nervously with loose change.

I watch quizzically as he shuffles off to his cave. I'll be damned. He's babysitting me. I shake my head in disbelief and get back to work in hopes that the rest of my day zips by. By five o'clock, I've conquered the inventory. Captain has me draw up a huge "Going out of Business" poster to hang in the window. Just like the old jerk to force me to do the dirty deed. It broke my heart to scrawl those words. I hang the sign in the front window and gather up my things, popping into Sutton's office to say goodbye to the old fart.

"Hey, I'm—what's wrong?" I freeze in my tracks when I see how pale he looks.

He glances over to me and shakes his head. "Nothing. It's that damn sandwich you fed me for lunch. I have indigestion from hell. Get me some antacids, will ya?"

I draw in a quiet breath of relief. I guess I kind of care about Captain a little, too. It's a love-hate thing, maybe. I've spent the last seven years of my life putting up with the old grump's bullshit, it would be normal to be a little attached right? I don't...love him or anything. He's my boss and I'm loyal is all. My silent ranting has my head spinning and even I have to admit that I'm trying to persuade myself that I don't care. I grunt in disgust with myself and snatch his antacids from behind the counter. I walk back into his office and plop two in his wrinkly palm. "There you are, oh Captain, my Captain. Anything else? Shall I spoon feed you now? Sponge bath?"

He narrows his blue eyes on me and grumbles a few obscenities while he chews up the chalky tablets.

"Better?"

"Yeah. Get out of here, you smart ass."

I snicker under my breath and stride out of his

office. I snatch up my bag and hightail it to my place in record time.

When I get to my apartment, I fire a text relaying my address to Damon. He responds right away with a simple *okay.* I strip off my jeans and graphic tee and hop into the shower, where I shave and exfoliate every inch of myself. I don't know why the hell I'm so damn compelled to get extra gussied up for him, but I do. I kind of want to impress him a little. Okay, a lot. I'm tied up in knots over this crap. This is not like me and it's infuriating! I shove away my irritation with myself and jump out of the shower, dry off and lotion up. I dart into my room and dig through my dresser in search of something lacey and sexy, finally slipping on a skimpy black thong and shoving my full breasts into the cups of a matching bra. Summer nights in Vegas make wardrobe choices simple: less is best. I quickly settle on a denim shorts and a teal tank, fasten the buckle on my gladiator sandals and check my ensemble in the mirror.

I approve. I scurry into my tiny bathroom and blow dry my wavy brown hair. I never style my hair. It's either down or in a ponytail. Honestly, I don't even know how to do all that fancy shit the other woman my age do. I grab my cosmetics and line my lids like normal, coat my lashes with mascara, and skip the blush, since I'm sure I won't need it. I pop my lips together after applying my tinted gloss and ruffle my hair a bit more, then snatch up my perfume and give my collar and wrist a spray. I hear a knock at my front door and my stomach clenches. Oh, geez. He's here. I give myself one more glance in the mirror and then make the short walk across my apartment to the front door. I swing it open and there he is. Damn, I don' think I'll ever tire of drinking in the sight of him. He's still in his gray suit and high-shine dress shoes. His hair is a little less disheveled and he's clean shaven. I guess he primped too. I wave him into my craphole apartment and get a whiff of his cologne as he passes by me. Panties on fire. I'm like a rabid dog in heat. I need to calm myself. I glance down and see he is holding a black wardrobe bag in his hands.

"What's that?" I ask with an arched eyebrow.

He smiles and unzips the bag. He reveals an amazing cocktail dress. I may not be fashion forward, but even I know a cocktail dress when I see one. This one is a single shoulder, satin dress that looks to be the size of a bandage. It's gorgeous.

"I am taking you to dinner and though I really, really, like those little shorts and tank top, you can't wear that where we're going." He fishes down into the bottom of the wardrobe bag and pulls out a pair of sky high stilettos and I instantly panic. I don't own a pair of stilettos and I doubt I know how to walk in them.

I shake my head vigorously. "The dress is beautiful, but there's no way in hell that I'm going to wear those heels."

He narrows his eyes and it only heightens my desire for him. "Yes, you are."

I cross my arms over my chest indignantly. "The hell I am!"

"And why won't you wear the heels?"

My puffed up indignation deflates and my shoulders slump fractionally. I hang my head, feeling stupid. How embarrassing is this? I'm twenty-five years old and have never worn heels that high. I can't just put those on and go out to dinner with him. I'll break my neck or at the very least, embarrass the hell out of both of us when I wobble all over the place. "I don't know how to walk in them," I mumble as my cheeks scorch red. I peek up at him.

He shoves the heels into the bag and sets it all across the back of my futon/couch. He steps forward and wraps me up in his arms; his smooth jaw brushes against my cheek as he whispers in my ear. "Don't worry about it. You can wear different heels tonight, but I promise you will learn how to walk in these fancy things. Understand?"

His words set me trembling. I can tell he's dead serious, and though he sounds all bossy and caveman macho, I find myself nodding my head in agreement. There's just something about his dominating personality that turns my insides into searing hot, pure arousal. I can feel the heat between my thighs. I'm a mess over him and honest to God, I have no desire to send him packing just yet.

"You're wet for me, aren't you?"

"Mhmm," I hum seductively.

"I know. I can smell you."

Holy fuck, that's hot.

He grips the nape of my neck with one hand and I close my eyes as the other skates down my body, flicking the button of my shorts open. He pulls the zipper down and they drop off my hips slightly. It's just enough space to allow him access. His hand slips into my shorts and I moan. He holds the nape of my neck, keeping my head from lolling forward to rest on that hard chest of his. His hand starts moving back and forth over my center.

"Open your eyes."

I pop my eyes open. We gaze at each other while he keeps up his movements. The pure heat and lust in his eyes has me ravenous for him.

"Let's skip dinner," I say in a pleading voice that

sounds alien to my own ears.

"I know what I plan on having to eat, what will you have?" His voice is husky and dripping with desire.

"You."

"Fine, if there's anything you need, I suggest you pack a bag."

I gape at him. What the hell does he mean, pack a bag? "A bag?"

"I told you, Jo. It's mine. All night. Let's go."

"Oh, yeah." I swallow hard and hurry to my bedroom. I grab a backpack from beneath my bed and toss in a bunch of random shit; I'm so flustered by him I can't think straight. I take a deep breath and dump out the bag on my bed. Let's try this again. I toss aside the bottle of aspirin and my bedside flashlight. What the fuck? Why am I rushing? I sigh and shake my head. He's being really bossy so he can wait a damn minute while I get my things. I calmly walk over to my dresser and pull out extra panties and another bra. I toss in a pair of jeans and another tank top. I dig into my nightstand for my birth control pills and shove them in, along with my cosmetic bag. With a zip, I sling the backpack onto my shoulder and walk back out to my small living room. Damon is waiting, the epitome of male yumminess, with his hands stuffed in his pockets as he casually surveys my apartment.

"I'm ready."

"Are you?" He winks slyly and scoops up the wardrobe bag; then, slipping the backpack off my shoulder, he transfers it to his and squeezes my hand.

"I am."

Chapter Nine

A Nobody

By the time we arrive at Damon's place, we're both anxious to get to his bedroom. He taps the button at the elevators and the doors chime as they slide open. He tugs me in, punches in a code, and we begin our ascent to the penthouse. The moment the doors close, he sweeps me up off my feet and my back crashes against the wall of the elevator. His full lips cover mine and his tongue plunders my mouth hungrily. I moan into him and he rolls his hips against mine. His cock is fighting to be freed, straining against his dress pants. The elevator lurches to a halt and the doors slide open. I'm set to my feet, then tugged by the hand to follow him. He hasn't said a damn thing since we left my place and I'm little nervous about it. Normally, no discussion would be a welcome thing for me, but something about Damon's silence has me feeling edgy. He unlocks the fancy door and pulls me into the penthouse. There's no hesitation and I'm immediately dragged to the stairs. I snatch my hand from his and pull away.

"Hey, are you okay?"

He sighs and rubs the bridge of his straight nose between his thumb and index finger. "Yes. I just—I want you. I have to have you." He exhales loudly and his chest deflates.

Oh. What does he mean he wants me and has to have me? If he's hinting at some type of long term thing, I can't give that to him. As much as I'd like to daydream about being normal and dating, falling in love and maybe even popping out a kid or two, it's just not in the plans for me. I'm not girlfriend material and I have no interest in setting myself up for more loss. Thanks, but no thanks.

I glance up into his warm, liquid honey eyes and I die a little on the inside. His eyes are brimming with need and desperation. Why me? I'm a nobody with nothing. Honestly, he shouldn't even be interested in me in any capacity other than casual sex a time or two. He's way out of my league. I wish I could be normal. If there was ever a man worth giving a shot it would be him, there's no doubt about it in my mind. I can't bring myself to ruin the mood, though. I'm a giant coward. It's wrong of me, but I decide to tell him what he wants to hear. It's a means to an end, and damnit, I want my end.

I love the way the veins on his long, muscular limbs stand out. Hot damn. He coils his gorgeous, strong arms around me and nuzzles my neck, laying a trail of hot kisses up to my ear.

"Wrap your legs around me."

I do as he says and he climbs the stairs two at a time, me clinging to him. Apparently this is his MO; not that I mind. A hot guy can carry me upstairs for a good fuck any time. I take the opportunity to inquire about our strange dilemma. "Anything come to mind? Any memories of me pop up?"

He pauses a long time and for a moment, I think maybe he hasn't heard me. "Only one thing *pops up* when I think about you, and you're about to find out what it is," he murmurs into my neck. I breathe an internal sigh of relief, knowing that our quest for answers gets to continue. He walks us down the corridor to his room and kicks open his door again; it's amazing that he hasn't put his foot through the damn thing. He takes me to his bed and plops me down.

"Wait." I hold up a hand, my palm resting against his thrumming chest. He freezes. I peek up at him and his face has gone blank, his pulse has sped up even further, and his skin is pale. What in the world? I push forward in spite of his odd behavior. "Don't you find it fucking odd as hell? This whole thing we feel? It's not normal. If I feel this connected to someone, shouldn't I have a memory of meeting them or knowing them? It's just odd, is all I'm saying. Are you sure you never volunteered or dropped off a donation at the mission?"

He inhales deeply. "No. I've never been there."

I shake my head and my brows draw together. This is driving me nuts. Maybe I feel like if somehow I sort out how I know him, the pull between us will be validated. "Maybe we were lovers in a past life or something," I say jokingly and shrug; he only half-smiles in response. What is his deal? "Are you sure you're okay?" I narrow my eyes on him skeptically. He's just acting so odd and I find it difficult to believe it's because he's eager to have me.

"I'd be better if we could stop talking and lose these clothes." He punctuates his statement with a light smack of his hand across my thigh. I yelp and he silences me with his skillful mouth. He pulls back, leaving me disgruntled over the loss of his lips against mine. He taps my forearm.

"Raise them."

I comply and lift my arms. He swiftly jerks my tank top over my head and tosses it to the floor. I'm sitting on the side of his bed in my bra, shorts, and sandals. He folds my hands together and sets them in my lap.

100

"Close your eyes, Josephine."

"It's Jo."

"No, it's not," he counters. The deep, authoritative tone in which he says it has me spellbound and lusting for him. He nips my neck and I lose all train of thought.

Suddenly, a soft fabric brushes over my face. I let out a gasp as he pulls the fabric snug across my eyes and ties it comfortably tight. I've never really been blindfolded during sex and I feel the tiniest bit of apprehension, but I know I can trust him, plus, this whole blindfold thing is hot. I'm in total darkness behind the cloth and I listen closely to him moving about. I hear his zipper lower and the shuffling of clothing. One of his hands cups my cheek and his thumb strokes a path across my cheekbone. He reaches behind me and snaps open my bra like he's done it a million times. Realistically, a man like Damon has likely had lots of playtime. I cringe at the thought of him with another woman. He slips my bra down my shoulders and I hear him toss it to the floor. He places a hand on each of my shoulders and gently pushes me until I'm flat on my back. My legs still dangle from the side of the bed and I'm still clothed from the waist down. I feel his hands glide down my legs then unclasp one sandal and then the other. They slip off with ease and I hear them hit the floor with a light thump. His warm hands envelope one of my feet and he kisses the instep, which is ticklish and erotic at the same time. It sends a charged current from the tips of my toes to my groin and my stomach clenches down low.

"Lift." He taps my hips and I prop my feet and the side rail of his bed, lifting my ass. His fingers hook into the waist of my shorts and panties and he drags them off, leaving me bare. His lips land on my stomach beneath my navel and I let out a breathy moan. He drops wet kisses up the center of my torso and then the bed dips and he's straddling me. One hand is lifted above me and he brings it to his lips, kissing my palm, then my wrist and all the way up my arm to the inside of my elbow, which sends that familiar current straight to my groin again. My arm is laid out above my head and he mirrors with my other. I feel him shift and leave the bed. What the hell?

"Where'd you go?"

"Hush. Patience."

I can hear him rustling around with something. What in the hell could he possibly be doing? Looking for a condom maybe? I feel the bed above my head dip and his mouth is against my ear.

"Are you still ready, Josephine?"

His warm breath against my skin makes me squirm and writhe involuntarily. I can feel the wetness between my thighs increase and my need for him grows ten-fold.

"Yes," I blurt eagerly.

"Tell me."

"I'm ready for you," I spit out in a rush. I feel an odd sense of shyness saying it, which is so unlike me. Shy is a foreign concept.

"Atta girl. This is going to be tight, but it won't hurt, I promise. I'd never hurt you."

"I know." Do I? My arms are extended out into a V above my head. I can feel him attach something like a cuff to each wrist. The material feels strong, but it's supple against my skin. There's a sudden zipping sound and my arms are stretched to their maximum, but he's right, it doesn't hurt in the slightest. My stomach feels like it's brimming with butterflies. He presses his lips to my cheek; I lean into his kiss and nuzzle him. I'm needy for contact. I want his skin on mine. All over mine. He fulfills me in a way no man ever has. When I'm near him, it seems like no other man exists, or ever has, that can compare. Maybe never will. I feel the brush of his leg beside mine. One of my feet is lifted and he slips on a heel. The stilettos. He guides my other foot into the dangerously high heel.

"I told you that you'd wear these heels tonight. Didn't I?"

"Yes," I quietly admit.

"Bend your knees for me, Baby." Baby? I've never

been called that before. Ok, maybe by some jackass catcalling a time or two, but never like this; never in a genuine way. It sends the butterflies in my stomach into a tailspin. I bend my knees and draw my legs up. The heels make it semi-awkward, but it feels so sexy. I'm tied up in nothing but stilettos and I feel all kinds of hot.

"Beautiful."

A small smile sneaks across my lips with his compliment. Both of his big, warm hands go to my thighs and I take in a shaky breath in anticipation. Damon's hands leave my skin no sooner than a moment after they were placed there, and I groan. A deep chuckle rumbles from him and it pisses me off. I'm getting impatient here. I'm tied up, naked, and waiting patiently. I don't think my pussy can get any wetter with arousal.

"Soon," is his answer to my petulant groan, "soon."

Another soft, yet strong, strap wraps around one thigh and then the other. Holy shit! He's tying up my legs so they stay in position. I'm not ready for this! As if he read my mind, he explains.

"It seems you have a slight inability to follow directions when my mouth is on that perfect pussy of yours, so I've remedied the situation. Now you can't move."

I draw in a breath and it does little to calm my eager

body.

"Are you still ready for me, baby?"

"Yes. Please."

"I'll be the judge of that."

One fingertip traces the moist seam of my opening and I tremble. He smoothes my arousal over me all the way down to my ass, I flinch a fraction at the intrusive touch.

"Perfect," he purrs. His hands grip both my ankles tightly and I can feel his mouth hovering above my needy core. His warm breath assails my hypersensitive flesh and I arch my back. Well, as much as I can arch my back when I'm secured to a bed. His broad bare shoulders rub against the inside of my knees as he leans forward and showers my stomach and hipbones with wet kisses. His tongue snakes out and licks a hot trail around my navel. I moan as my hips fight against the bonds to move forward to him. "You have no patience, baby. We'll have to work on that."

"You mean torture and tease me until I stop?" I snap like an errant child.

"Would you like to be gagged, too?"

"No," I mumble.

"That's good. I would sure dislike having to gag you. That mouth of yours makes some of the most seductive sounds when I'm buried to the hilt."

Oh, fuck my life! This man is going to be the death of me. His lips land on the inside of one of my knees and he plants a lingering soft kiss there.

"I." He moves further up my trembling leg and plants another soft kiss.

"Love." Higher yet again and another kiss that has me tugging in vain against my bonds.

"That." His lips linger against the joint between my pussy and my upper thigh. I moan and pant in desperation.

"Mouth." His silky tongue makes contact with my clit and he makes one painfully slow lick from my clit all the way to my ass, making me gasp and squirm. His muscular arms wrap around each of my upper thighs and hold me even more immobile, holding my legs in a vice like grip and I'm left vulnerable to his ministrations. His tongue twirls around the perimeter of my opening and my body clenches fiercely.

"Mmmm," I hum appreciatively.

His mouth is the most divine thing I've ever experienced and I swear, I've never been pleasured so thoroughly. He makes another slow pass from top to bottom and I moan. His lips seal around my clit and he alternates between flicks of his tongue and strong suckling.

"Damon," I grind out through my pleasure.

His exquisite mouth leaves my clit and his attention goes to my slick opening. His tongue plunges deep then withdraws. He works me in this fashion until every breath is a moan. I can barely breathe and he has easily and skillfully worked me to climax. I feel my mounting pleasure tightening up low in my stomach. He stops. My orgasm slips through my fingers and I whimper. One finger dives deep into me. He draws it out and smoothes my wetness over my ass. I once again flinch at the intrusive feeling of his touch against such a private place. I've had plenty of sex, but anal play isn't something I've ventured into. He presses a finger to the tight bud and I do my best to relax. One long finger slips into my channel. Now a second finger. His knowing touch builds me to orgasm in no time.

"Ahh," I suck in air through gritted teeth and moan.

"Relax," he says from between my legs.

His breath against my flesh sets fire to my sensitive nerve endings. His mouth covers my clit again and resumes his previous flicking and suckling. His two fingers ease in and out in short rubbing strokes against the front wall of my pussy. His thumb circles the tight virgin bud of my ass once more before breaching past the tight ring of muscle. I gasp in shock and my eyes bulge behind my blindfold. I pull against the restraints that are keeping me open to him.

"Relax, baby," he repeats, his mouth still pressed to my clit.

I'm trying my best to do as he says. He continues working me so completely; I can feel my stomach coiling tighter. His thumb applies just the right amount of pressure against the flesh separating his fingers and thumb. It feels exotic and intrusive and stimulating. Every nerve is firing and I feel like I could combust.

"Oh, Damon, don't stop. Don't stop," I moan loudly.

A low growl emanates from his chest sending a vibrating sensation through my groin and it sends me into a shaking, erupting fit of climactic pleasure. My limbs shake and shudder as they jerk against the ties that bind me. I gasp for air and it takes me a long moment before I am able to draw in a full breath. I hear a zip noise again and he has slackened the ties that hold each leg apart. There's another zip, which I assume is the sound of the rope being adjusted, and suddenly I'm free of the bindings. My limbs relax and rest lifelessly against the bed. I pant and work at gathering myself. The bed dips and I can feel heat radiating from his body. He straddles me and lifts me at the nape, sliding the blindfold off. I blink to clear away the blurry vision and he comes into focus above me. Holy fuck, I feel like I'm seeing him for the first time. His amber eyes are on fire and his cheeks have just a tinge of pink; his nearly-black hair is a delicious-looking mess. I want to prop up on an elbow so I can run my fingers through it, but I'm still recovering from that heavenly orgasm. His chest is bare and I yearn to touch it. I lift my head enough to peer between my thighs and he is just as naked as me. His formidable erection hovers above the place I want it most.

He leans down, threads one arm between my back and the mattress and lifts me to his chest, bringing me to a kneeling position that mirrors his. The tip of his bare cock butts against my stomach. His gaze is piercing and intense, almost uncomfortably so. I search for a reprieve and find it, looking down to relish the sight of his length pressing against me. I'm so enamored, no, distracted, by the sight that I have the first careless thought I've ever had with regards to sex: I imagine taking control. I imagine pushing him back and gliding over that beautiful piece of completely natural, bare man. I shove aside the idiotic idea and glance back up to him. I swear, he must know exactly what thoughts flit through my brain, because a crooked smile tilts the edge of his lips. He shifts our position so that he's sitting with his back is to the headboard, looking like the King of the manor. He motions his chin towards his nightstand. I sprawl across his big bed, dig into the drawer, and toss him a condom.

"You know, I won't use these forever." He holds up the condom and I just look from him to the condom then back to him. "One day I'm going to take you bare. You'll be the first woman I've ever had without a condom."

Oh fuck, he makes the temptation all the more difficult to resist.

"Have you ever not used protection?"

I shake my head no. "I'm clean," I offer up. What the fuck? Why do I sound like I'm trying to convince him? He arches an eyebrow. Holy shit, I think he's just going to take my word for it.

"So am I."

I believe it. I don't know why, I just do. It's dumb as hell. I have to get this condom on him or we'll end up acting on that dumbass idea right now. I snatch back the condom and rip it open with my teeth. He gives me another crooked smile as I pull the rolled latex from its wrapper.

"One day...soon."

I ignore him and roll the condom over the tip and down his thick shaft. He watches me and it's a little unnerving. The moment the protection is in place, he wraps his arms around my waist and jerks me to him.

"Wrap your legs around me," he orders, and I

comply. He's still sitting and now I'm straddling his lap with my legs around his waist. I glance between us and his cock is jutting upward, resting against my stomach, I can feel his pulse thrumming through his erection. One arm leaves my waist and his hand tangles into my hair. He pulls me forward and rests his head against mine. I peek through my lashes. His eyes are closed and he looks like he's in pain. I knew something was wrong.

"What's wrong?" I cup his angular jaw and force him to look at me.

His eyes open lazily. His grip around my waist tightens and all at once, he lifts me. His ready cock slips into position and he swiftly he pulls me down onto him, making me gasp at the fullness and invasion. My head lolls forward to rest on his shoulder.

"Nothing's wrong now," he purrs in my ear.

I keep my hand on his jaw and turn my head to nuzzle his neck and lay my lips on every exposed inch of skin I can reach. I begin to rock my hips slowly back and forth, grinding hard against his cock. He groans as I move over him. I want to speed up, but going this slow is driving him crazy. I can tell he wants to hammer into me like he did last night.

"Fuck," he roars, then flips me to my back, his erection still fully sheathed within my body.

I gasp as my back hits the mattress. How did he *do* that? His fingers thread into my hair and pull my mouth to his; our lips crash together and our tongues tangle. I can taste myself on his tongue, and fuck, it turns me wild.

"Fuck me," I breathe.

He pulls back, slowly withdrawing his glistening wet length. He slams back into me and I let out a loud moan. He withdraws once more. Just the tip remains and he slams into me again, stealing my breath. His warm eyes stay locked onto mine and I almost melt on the spot. I know him, but I don't. I want him, but I don't. I need him, but I don't. His pace quickens as he withdraws again and again, burying his cock hard within me with each thrust.

"Oh fuck," I moan as he jackhammers into me, unrelentingly. My nails dig into his shoulders. His skin mists over with sweat; it beads and rolls down his brow, then drips to my sternum. His muscles begin to tense even more as he grunts and plows through me.

"Oh, fuck, baby," he growls through gritted teeth.

My stomach tightens and my muscles clench his cock. My pussy throbs and spasms as another mind blowing orgasm rips through me. "Damon!" I scream. The moment his name tears from my throat, he rams himself into me as far as he can. He stills, buried to the hilt, and shudders over and over as my body milks his shaft for every last drop of his pleasure. He collapses onto me, and though he is far too heavy for me to breathe deeply, I wrap my legs around him and stroke my fingertips across his back as we work to catch our breath.

"Are you on birth control?" he murmurs, his mouth against my neck.

What the hell? Apparently he *is* serious about not using a condom.

"Yes," I answer honestly.

"What kind?"

"The pill."

"No more condoms."

"Bullshit! You aren't going to decide that on my behalf."

He kisses my neck and props himself on his elbows. Those amber eyes cut into me like a heated scalpel. "You may not realize it yet, but you're mine. Not because I'm claiming you. You're mine because that's how it is. I feel like I've waited my whole life to find you. Before we met in that store, I dreamed of you every night; I wondered where you were and when I'd find you. Now that I have, you'd be crazy if you think I'd just let you go. I don't see a need for protection. I don't want a damn thing between us." He kisses me breathless before withdrawing himself and disappearing into the bathroom.

My heart skips a beat in my chest and I know my jaw hangs open. I take a deep breath and count to ten. What does that mean? For me? For us? Is there an us? I don't even know what to say to that. He strides back into the room, giving me a full, uninhibited view of his glorious naked body. I watch him shamelessly. He crawls into the bed with me and takes his place between my legs again. His chest covers my stomach and his head rests on my sternum, arms wrapping around me and his big hands cupping my ass. I can't help but thread my fingers through his dark hair; it slips like silk through my fingers. I take another deep, exasperated breath. I don't know what the hell I've gotten myself into with him, but I can't deny that what he said. I, too, feel like I've been waiting for him without even knowing it. I, too, feel the connection that says I could never want another man the way I want him. But I also know that I'm not the dating type; I don't even know how to be someone's girlfriend.

"We barely know each other. What do you want with me? And don't say you want to figure out if we've met before, because that would be a big-ass lie and you know it."

"I know enough about you and I'll tell you anything you want to know. It may be asking a lot of you, but I would regret never trying. Just give this a chance. Give me a chance; agree to be mine. Exclusively."

"Are you asking me to be your girlfriend?"

"I am," he huffs out.

I sigh dramatically and I feel his muscles tense against me. Is he nervous? "I can't make any promises, but I'll think about it." My heart pounds out of control in my chest and I can feel that his is doing the same. I think I'm in an impossible position here. I'm freaked the hell out and excited at the same time. I feel his lips curve up into a smile and for a moment, I want to shout "yes!" He's amazing and I'd be a damn fool to not scream "yes!" from the mountain tops. I'm so fucked up. I run soothing hands through his hair and he sighs, content with my promise to think about it; it's not long before Damon is out cold.

Chapter Ten

Small Miracles

For the second morning in a row, I'm awakened by the relentless ringing of my cell phone.

"Ugh!" I groan and roll out of Damon's plush bed, stumble to my phone and answer it grumpily. "What?"

Sutton laughs into the phone which only furthers my irritation. "Good morning to you too, Miss USA."

I roll my eyes. I'll never live down that damned nickname. I suppose he will never live down Captain either. "What now?" I ask gruffly, glancing at the clock. Nine o'clock. Damn, I slept late.

"Good news, Jo."

Those words have me wide eyed and awake in a nanosecond. I rub away the sleep and wait for the good news.

"You won't be coming in today. I have an offer on

the store and I'm gonna take it. Someone is buying the place."

"What?!" I screech. I can't believe this. I suppose it's good news for him, but in my opinion, I'd rather the damn place remain vacant instead of flipped to a fucking chintzy gag store or something.

"Yep. I have a meeting with the buyer today. So I'll call you once it's done and fill you in on the details."

"Okay." I hang up, defeated. I hate having to just eat shit and grin. I glance back to the bed and notice that Damon is gone, but I could care less at the moment. I just want to climb my stark naked ass into that bed and sleep all day. I suppose the responsible thing to do would be to job hunt, but I just don't give a shit right now. I mope back to the bed, pull the covers up to my ears, close my eyes, and drift.

"Josephine," he whispers.

I startle and jerk upright, smashing my forehead right into his mouth. "Ah, shit," I yell and rub my palm against my forehead.

"You have a hard head, don't you?"

I open my eyes and glance to Damon. I gasp. "Oh crap, you're bleeding. Shit, I'm sorry. You scared me. Stay there." I jump up and hurry to get a towel from the bathroom. I dampen the corner under the cool water and return to a sinfully handsome, but bleeding, Damon. He's sitting on the edge of the bed with his shiny dress shoes perched on the rail. I position myself between his knees and hold the cloth to his busted lip.

"I'm sorry," I whisper, carefully wiping the blood away from his bottom lip.

"I didn't mean to scare you. I just thought I should wake you. You've been sleeping all day."

I crane my neck to see the clock. Shit! I have been sleeping all day. It's after one o'clock in the afternoon. My stomach rumbles embarrassingly and he chuckles.

"I thought you might be hungry. I guess I was right." His hands glide over my hips and settle on my ass, reminding me that I'm still naked. His big hands cup my cheeks and pull me closer to him. Why is he dressed like this? It's a Saturday.

"It's Saturday."

"Yes. And?" he says as his lips land on my collarbone. He kisses across my chest.

"Why are you dressed like that?"

His hands squeeze my ass cheeks. I drop the towel to the floor and wrap my arms around his neck.

"Work never ends for me. No such thing as a day off." One hand leaves my ass to cup my breast. He covers my taut nipple with his hot mouth and I suck in a breath of air.

"No rest for the weary and all that jazz," I quip breathily.

"Precisely."

"You're going to hurt your lip again doing all that."

"Can't think of a better reason to hurt," he mumbles against my skin as he moves across to the other breast. He kisses and suckles my nipple then releases me. "Thank you."

"For?"

"For being such a devoted nurse." He smiles a heart-melting, playful smile, looking light years different than the serious man I slept with last night.

I'd give just about anything to get inside that handsome head of his.

"You're a top notch patient, so I can't complain." I smile back at him.

He takes in a deep breath and sighs. There it is again. Something is going through that head of his and I wish like hell he'd just spit it out already.

"What?"

"Oh nothing, I was just thinking I should probably stop before I tie you to my bed for the rest of the day," he says, just as casual as can be.

I snap my head back and clutch my stomach as I

laugh harder than I can ever remember laughing. "Y-you think you're gonna keep me in bed all day?" I sputter out between gasps.

"Watch me, Baby. Now, get dressed. Let's go eat." His big paw smacks my ass hard and makes a clap so loud that I flinch and pulls me to my feet. I guess my day is free, so why the hell not go have lunch with him?

"Where are my clothes?" I scan the floor for my abandoned shorts and tank, but they're nowhere to be found. I arch one brow quizzically.

He stands from the bed and slips his hands into his pants pockets. "Yesterday, before I came to get you, I had Brian go shopping. According to him, every gay man has an eye for fashion. The things he and the saleslady chose arrived this morning. I brought them in while you were sleeping." He flicks his chin towards an open set of French doors. "It's in the closet."

"Oh." It's such a presumptive thing to do, and part of my brain says I should be irritated with his forwardness, but I'm so shocked that he bought me anything I don't know how to respond.

"Why would you do that? We just met. You can't just throw a bunch of money and stuff at me. I don't need any handouts."

He shrugs, then strides over to where I am standing

still with not a stitch of clothing covering me. He pulls me to him and holds my gaze. "I want you to understand something, Josephine. When I say something, I mean it. I meant what I said last night. I want you. I'd be crazy to let you go. If you just give me the chance, I'll win you over. You'll realize this isn't just some hookup. I want to make you comfortable and happy. I'm not asking your permission, Josephine." He turns me by my shoulders and steers me to the massive walk-in closet, directing me to a rack of clothing.

"I can't repay you for these things," I say softly, looking away. I'm embarrassed to admit just how poor I am. I have no savings and my belongings are limited.

"The only thing I want from you is you."

"I-"

He interrupts my protest. "You think you can't give that to me, but I'm going to prove you wrong. Let me prove you wrong, Josephine."

The pleading in his voice rings loud and clear. Damnit! I'm not used to caring about other people; why am I so emotional right now? It has to be the timing of all this. The closing of the store in such close proximity to the anniversary of the accident is what's got me emotional. Yeah, that's it. I lift my hand and run it across the long row of clothes hanging in front of me. Unwelcome tears sting the backs of my eyes. No one has ever been so...nice to me. Not that I deserve anything nice, but still.

He grasps my chin forcing me to look at him. "Don't cry, they're just clothes. No big deal."

I swipe at my stupid big tears. "No one has ever given me anything. Sutton gave me an outfit to work in, but he was a real dick about it. and you...you're just giving me this shit and it's a lot more than I deserve. I ju-"

His grip on my chin tightens and I shut my mouth. "I don't want to hear that from you ever again, do you understand?"

I give a tiny nod.

"No. Say you understand." His voice is stern and I impulsively listen and do as he says. It's beyond annoying.

"I understand."

"You are an amazing woman who's had a fucked up life because of some irresponsible asshole. That man's actions have hurt you in unimaginable ways. I want to make it right. Had those things never happened, I bet you would've had a very different life. You deserve so much and I intend to give you those things."

Oh. My. God. This man has got to be a fucking dream. I don't deserve shit, but he thinks I do. I've got to give this crazy thing between us a go. I'll regret it if I don't. Tears build in my eyes double time and spill over. He wipes them away and holds me to him. I don't know how or why I was put in his path, but I'm glad for it. I think he may be the best thing that's happened to me since the accident. I run my hands over my sodden face and take a deep cleansing breath.

"Okay," I say with a tone of finality.

"Okay?" He holds me by the shoulders and draws back to get a look at me.

"Yeah, okay." I repeat.

"Okay to the clothes?"

"Okay to...you know," I shrug and flick a wrist, pointing in no specific direction.

"I mean okay, I'll be your...your—"

"Girlfriend? You'll date me?" His face lights up, and fuck if it doesn't make my apprehension vanish into thin air. He is something else.

"Yes."

"Exclusively?"

"I sure as hell hope so," I snap.

"Good, because I will not share you with any other man." He looks at me squarely and I absorb the sense of peace and satisfaction in his eyes. It's raw and disarming. "Ever. I can make you happy."

I believe him, too. I don't know how, but something in me tells me that he can and he will. I may be an idiot for believing him, but the alternative is not an option. I'll give him, give us a chance. "I know you can," I say softly.

His lips lift into just a fraction of a smile. "I put the rest in that dresser." He points to an island dresser like I've seen in one of those fancy-ass home magazines. There are two of them in the middle of this living room-sized closet.

"There's more in there?"

He smiles and nods. I look around in awe. I can't even wrap my brain around this. I have a tiny little closet that is barely full. I have thrift store clothing mostly, since I refuse to pay much for a pair of jeans or a top. I guess, if nothing else, my time on the streets taught me how to be frugal.

"Yes. Though I like the idea of you being panty-less around me, I won't deny you undergarments," he jokes. I smack his arm playfully and he sweeps me up to him again, laying another breathtaking kiss on me. He breaks away and rests his cheek against mine. "I need to feed you, and then I have something I want to discuss, but take your time, baby." He releases me and smacks my ass, then leaves me alone in the massive closet.

I should shower before dressing in these fancy clothes. I walk out of the closet and into his resort-style bathroom. I swing open the door to the shower. "What the hell?" I moan. How do you turn this thing on? There are multiple sprayer thingies and a few different controls. Who in the hell decided to screw up taking a shower by complicating it? I fiddle with the taps until finally warm water shoots from just the main shower head above me. Thank fuck for small miracles. I use his products and I can't say I mind in the slightest. I like the smell of his soap. It makes me think of him. I'll have to remind myself not to sniff my own arm all day like some jonesing crackhead. I laugh at my inner musings and towel off. I enter the closet again and pull open one of the dresser drawers. Panty heaven! There must be dozens of panties here in all types and colors. I dig through the undergarments like a kid on Christmas. Lace. Cotton. Silk. Boyshorts. Thongs. G-Strings. Bikinis. I sigh as I choose a pair of beige lace boyshorts. I pull them on, reveling in the delicious, silky feel, and find a black lace bra in the next drawer. I open another drawer and it's full of those garter things with the nylons. I don't know what in the hell he expects me to do with those. I've never even worn them before. The next two drawers have lingerie, nightgowns, and pajamas in every style, fabric and color imaginable.

"Wow," I say to myself. I walk back to the rack of clothing, scanning the garments. My sights set on a navy, chiffon shell top. I've seen things like this, but I don't own anything like it; it's gorgeous. I quickly locate a white camisole and slip a really nice pair of white linen shorts with a cuffed hem over my hips. I slide the shell over my shoulders and button it, suddenly feeling strangely "put together." Maybe I'm on one of those prank shows and someone's going to pop out of the enormous shoe rack and burst my bubble. This can't really be happening. I sit down and finger comb my brown waves, trying to get a grip. I lean forward and grab a box from the bottom shelf of the rolling rack and flip the lid off.

"Jimmy Sh-shoo? Hmm." I pull a metallic heel from the box. It's gorgeous and way fancier than any of the secondhand shit in my closet. I put the lid back in place and grab the rest of the boxes. I line them up and flip the lids on all of them.

"Jimmy Shoo. Jimmy Shoo. Jimmy Shoo. Jimmy Shoo." Who is this Jimmy cat?

"Damon!" I shout like a mad woman. Nothing. "DAMON!" I hear some fumbling, and a second later, Damon barrels into the closet with wide eyes. Ah, shit. I scared him.

"What's wrong? Why are you on the floor?" He sounds panicked and I feel like a total asshole. I yell for Sutton all the time and he for me. I guess it's a habit.

"Sorry." I cringe. He visibly relaxes.

"I was just wondering about these." I hold up a glittery pump and his brows shoot up.

"Okay, but I doubt I can tell you very much about women's footwear."

I click my tongue at his smartass remark. "No, I was wondering about the brand. Who is Jimmy Shoo?"

He laughs at me and I throw the heel at him, which he catches with little effort. "Okay, I'm a guy and even I know that Jimmy Choo is a designer. The ladies like his stuff," he explains.

"Oh. Choo as in chew. Got it. These look expensive. How much were they?" I slip on a pair of navy cork wedge sandals. I'm glad to see a few pairs of wedges since they're the only type of heel I know how to walk in. I only have a few pairs of shoes and one pair of wedge sandals. These are really nice. I'm feeling all kinds of spoiled right now and I'm kind of loving it.

"It doesn't matter the price," he answers and I cock a brow as I stand.

"How much, Damon?"

"Doesn't matter, Josephine."

I cross my arms over my chest and prop out a sandal clad foot. "Tell me or I'm going home," I threaten.

His eyes widen. "No, you aren't. I'm keeping you." He strides over to me and my mound of shoes, bends purposefully down and tosses me over his shoulder. I squeal and slap his ass from my upside down position. A low laugh rumbles from his throat as he totes me from the bedroom and down the stairs to the kitchen. I laugh as he flips me upright and sits me down on the countertop.

"What can we make to eat, woman?"

"Let's not make a mess. We can go to The Diner."

"What diner?"

"The Diner. That's what it's called." I shrug. "I go there for breakfast before work every day. It's cheap and their coffee is the best. They make great cheeseburgers, too."

"The Diner it is."

"You have to change your clothes, though. It's not a suit and tie kind of place."

"Only if you help me."

"I think I can arrange that." I give him a naughty smile and know I'm in trouble. He growls as he tosses me back over his shoulder and heads towards the stairs.

Chapter Eleven

Let's Talk

I explain where The Diner is and we make the trip across town in comfortable silence. His hand crosses the console of his fancy Beamer and claims a spot on my thigh. He looks over at me and squeezes as he smiles, exposing his pearly white teeth. It successfully melts my indifferent heart. Damon does something to me and I don't know what the hell to think of it. I'm out of sorts, but I'm kind of enjoying it. I don't feel so alone with him. I feel like I belong somewhere, with someone. It's a revelation in my screwed up world.

He parks right in front and jumps out and walks around to my side of the car to open my door. Someone pinch me. He has got to be joking. No one holds open doors for me. I sit and admire how great he looks in his jeans, snug white tee and Chucks. He's gorgeous, whether he's in a suit and tie or his plain casual clothes. His warm, amber eyes seem to glow in the sunlight and his thick, dark hair flutters in the light breeze.

"Are you going to get out or should I bring your food to the car?"

I snap out of my ogling and step out. "Sorry, I was enjoying the view."

He sweeps my hand from my side and threads our fingers together. I freeze and he tugs me along. "This is what couples do. They hold hands. Eat lunch together. You'll get used to it." He gives my hand a squeeze.

We step into The Diner and I point to my usual booth. We slide into the worn bench seat and I wave at Noni. She catches my gesture out of the corner of her eye as she scoops ice into a cup and I watch as her jaw drops. Yep, Noni, I brought a man with me. She whips out her order pad and pencil and all but runs to us.

"Hey, Noni," I say casually.

"Hey, doll." She looks to Damon and stares. What the hell, Noni? He's a bit young for you. Noni's got to be in her fifties, but I guess she could be a cougar. I wouldn't doubt it. She's a beautiful middle-aged woman. Her dark brown hair is sprinkled generously with gray, but she wears it well. Crow's feet mar the edges of her almond-shaped, hazel eyes. But overall, she's aged gracefully, which is really saying something for a woman who's busted her ass as a waitress for all of her adult life.

"Noni, this is my -"

"Boyfriend," Damon interjects as he shoves his arm forward. Noni extends her hand to him and they shake.

"Damon, this is Noni. I see her about as much as I see Sutton."

"Damon Cole, it's a pleasure to meet the woman who feeds my lady breakfast." Damon winks at her, showing off his winning smile.

I roll my eyes as I watch Noni's face pale and her hands tremble. Really? Dear, God, Non, get a hold of yourself.

"Damon Cole," she mutters. Okay, this is awkward.

"Alrighty then," I say, feigning enthusiasm as I drum my fingers on the table. "Now that the introductions are out of the way... I'm starving, what about you?" I look to Damon.

"I'll have whatever you're having." Smart man.

"Okay, that's fair enough. So then we'll take two cheeseburgers with bacon, double patty for Big Man here, cut the lettuce, tomato, and onion, mayo for me, and..." I arch a brow at Damon.

"Mustard," he adds.

"Mustard for him, two orders of fries, and two

waters. No lemon." I cap off our order with a smile and Noni walks away, scribbling.

"How long have you been coming here?"

I take a deep breath and think back. "Right after I started working at the store, so seven years I guess."

He nods. "Nice place."

"So, what was it that you wanted to talk to me about?"

He begins to open his mouth, but is cut off by my damned phone. I dig the phone out and Sutton's name on the screen. I swear, the old fart is the only one who ever calls me. It's a testament to how lackluster my life really is. Was. Whatever. I swipe my thumb across the screen and hold it to my ear.

"What's up, Captain?" I glance to Damon and watch him purse his lips together and pinch the bridge of his nose. What the hell is wrong now?

"Have you talked to that boyfriend of yours?"

I scowl at his tone. "He isn't my boyfriend!" I clip into to phone. I glance up to Damon. He's pissed. Fuck. His eyes narrow on me and I feel pinned to this seat. I need to get off the phone and explain.

"Well, if he isn't your boyfriend now, he will be when I tell you that he's the one who bought the store. That man seems to be set on impressing you, Miss USA."

"I'll call you back," I mumble and quickly hang up.

"Not your boyfriend, huh?"

I stare at him blankly. I don't know what the hell to make of what Sutton said about Damon being the buyer. Why would he do that? I don't even know what to say to him. Noni interrupts our silent staring match; she sets the plates down and nearly trips over her own feet trying to get away from us.

"You bought the store?"

He looks up from his food. "We'll talk about this when we get back to my place." His voice is firm and intimidating.

I must've really pissed him off. I press forward anyway. "No, I want to talk about it now."

He closes his eyes and takes in a deep breath. He opens them and his fiery gaze burns into me. "No. We will discuss this when we get back, Josephine." He waves two fingers in the air to signal Noni for the check and she delivers it, along with two to-go boxes. He loads up both of our meals and tosses a one-hundred dollar bill on the table, slipping out of the booth and dragging me towards the car.

Our ride back to his place is silent, but far from comfortable. When we get into the elevator, he jabs his finger angrily into the panel. Why the hell is he so quiet? I need to explain why I said that to Sutton and he needs to explain what the hell is going on with the store. The elevator comes to a stop and the doors open. He still hasn't said a word. My hand is swept from my side and tugged forward. He opens the front door and pulls me behind him. I try pulling away, but his grip only tightens. I wish he would just stop and say something. The silence is unnerving.

"Are you going to say anything? Tell me what's going on?"

"Baby, I'm about to tell you everything you need to know. Trust me." I'm dragged up the staircase so fast my feet can barely keep pace with his. He leads us into the library and I'm even more confused. Are we seriously going to sit down and talk things over in the fucking library like two stuffy business associates?

"Take off your clothes, Josephine," he orders in a low, demanding voice.

"What?" My brows bunch together.

"Take off your clothes or I'll take them off for you, but it's doubtful that they'll be wearable, once I'm done."

I stand frozen in place, shocked and confused at his words. I don't understand why he won't just talk about this shit.

"Fine," he huffs as he strides forward to me. He

grips the delicate fabric of the navy shell and rips it open.

"My shirt!" I gasp.

His hands go to the hem of my camisole and he muscles it open as well. What the hell? His destructive hands go to the waistband of my shorts and rip! Fuck! I'm left in my panties and bra before him.

"Talking seems a lot more productive then tearing up clothes, don't you think?" I grate through gritted teeth.

"Ready to talk, Josephine?"

What? I'm so confused. I furrow my brows again and begin to shake my head.

"Let's talk, baby," he purrs in my ear.

Oh shit. My stomach flips and flutters as I grasp what he intends on doing. I can't say I don't want it. I could use an orgasm or two, or three.

He clasps my bra and easily snaps it open; it falls to the floor. The delicate lace of my underwear is no match for his brute force. He demolishes them with one forceful yank. "Now we talk."

I say nothing in return. I'm speechless and turned on by this amazing, multi-faceted man.

His fingers brush my elbow and guide me behind one of the oversized plush chairs. "Bend over and ready yourself, baby."

Ready myself for what? My hands develop a small

tremor and I lean forward over the chair, as instructed. I peek back over my shoulder and see him shed his clothing. My core tightens with anticipation. The heat between my legs burns white hot as my arousal builds. His big hand lands on the back of my neck and gives a brief squeeze before trailing down my spine. One finger slips between my cheeks and lingers, trailing down the seam of my opening. I close my eyes and revel in the feel of his touch. The tearing of foil catches my attention and I'm glad that the condom discussion has been saved for another time. The head of his erection nudges against my opening. He carefully and gently guides the tip of himself into me. I breathe deeply in anticipation. He moves in further, just a fraction.

"Who are you, Josephine?" he asks in a calm yet lusty voice.

I see what he's playing at. "I'm your girlfriend," I answer, feeling a little proud of myself.

"If you're my girlfriend, then what does that make me, Josephine?" he punctuates his sentence by filling me with the full length of his cock all at once. I gasp and involuntarily rock up onto my tiptoes. His strong hands hold my hips tightly and I struggle to fill my lungs. He withdraws slowly.

"Tell me."

Once again, he plows into me, stealing my breath in the most delicious way. My body clenches in pleasure.

"My boyfriend." My voice comes out weak and breathy.

"Say it again," he orders.

I comply on yet another hard thrust. "Ah! My boyfriend."

He rears back and comes at me again. The head of his cock bangs away at the deepest parts of me, sending exquisite little aches through my womb. "Again," he pants.

"My boyfriend!" I shout.

His speed increases and he pounds me to climax in no time. One hand leaves my hip to reach around and massage my breast. He groans in appreciation. I feel his body tense as he nears orgasm along with me. I pant hard and start seeing spots. My stomach clenches. My channel tightens around his perfect cock. A lightning storm of raw pleasure rips through my veins as my orgasm consumes me. He stills, buried deep, and shudders; a guttural groan resonates through his chest. His fingers dig into my flesh while our bodies are overcome with the perfect synchronicity of breathtaking ecstasy. He rests his forehead against my back, pulls out of me, and stands me upright to face him.

"I didn't mean it," I say on a rush. "I only said it

because of Sutton. I don't want to hear any shit from him."

"I'd never deny you. Please don't deny me."

Oh damn, now I feel like a real douchebag. He sounds wounded and I'm to blame. Who cares if Sutton knows? I can handle his old ass. I won't be able to hide my relationship with Damon forever.

"Why'd you buy the store? Are you going to turn it into a bar or something?"

"Look around yourself," he orders.

I do. I scan the library. My eyes flit over the rows and rows of books around me. I look back to him and quirk up an eyebrow. So what does he want me to see?

"Books are what you love. They're what you know. It's obviously your passion. I didn't want you to lose that; you've lost enough." His voice is low and velvet smooth in my ears.

My heart squeezes and aches in my chest. I feel the sting of tears threatening. "What?" I whisper barely loud enough to hear.

Those honey eyes cut into me. He grips my shoulder with one hand and runs the backside of the other over my jaw. "You've lost enough. I bought the store for you. I want you to run it. It's in your hands now."

"You didn't buy it so you'd have some kind of control over me?"

The corner of his lips lifts into a small smirk. "I'd be lying if I said that purchasing the store in no way benefitted me." His big, bare shoulders rise and fall as he shrugs. "I figured it's the way to my lady's heart. So I bought the place."

Without hesitation, I wrap my arms around his middle and breathe a deep sigh of relief.

"I...I..."

"Hush." He lifts a finger and holds it to my lips, effectively silencing me. "I told you I'd give you what you deserve. Let me show you." He bends at the waist and sweeps me off my feet, pulling me tight against his defined chest and down the wide corridor to his bedroom.

I feel as if I'm in some type of euphoric daze and I have to admit, I've never felt so lucky in my life. It doesn't feel like we met yesterday. His generosity doesn't feel like charity. It feels like something good and genuine and beautiful, and it's mine as long as I take what he offers. I can't refuse him. Not in any capacity.

Chapter Twelve

Something To Be Proud Of

"I don't get it. Why me? You're way out of my league."

He sets me down on his bed and climbs over the top to lie down beside me, wrapping his arms around my bare body and tugging me into his chest. It's quickly becoming my favorite place to be. I feel so safe here. I feel...right, being here. Right here in his arms. It's so damn confounding. I peek over my shoulder at Damon and see his warm eyes on me.

"I can't explain it. I saw you and everything came together for the first time in my life. It felt like breathing. You're the one who's out of my league. I don't deserve you. Trust me."

Why would he say that? Even hearing it makes me ache for him. I turn in his arms to face him.

"You...you are amazing in every way! How in the hell could you possibly not deserve me? I just hope by some miracle I can really be what you think I am."

"I know I'm right about you. I can feel it. My gut is never wrong."

"You're kind of cocky and a whole lot bossy, Big Man," I muse tauntingly. He cocks up a brow and smiles a panty-dissolving, pearly white, crooked smile. Damn, I'm in so much trouble with him. How have my underwear not spontaneously combusted by now? I never knew I could feel this happy around someone. I could easily fall for him. Hell, maybe I already am.

His fingers crawl up my ribs then tickle me beneath my arms.

"Stoooooooooop!" I squeal like a wounded animal and flail about.

"Aw, my Josephine can't stand to be tickled," he teases and he keeps at it; I squirm and bat at him.

"Pleeeease!" I cry out.

His hands leave my sides as he lifts his big body and swings a leg over me, rolling me to my back. He straddles me and pulls my arms above my head, holding me immobile with ease. My smile fades as I look up into those pools of warm honey. I like being here. I enjoy being with him. I don't know how I could ever *not* have him. What if this doesn't go anywhere? What if it doesn't last?

"What's wrong?" A deep crease mars his forehead, his concern evident.

I sigh and clear my throat to confess my worries. I feel like I can talk to him about it. I should talk to him about it. "I'm scared." I admit my fear honestly and watch as he purses his lips together. "I'm scared that if I get attached to you, I'll be destroyed if something ever happened to us or to you. I won't put myself in a position to lose again. I would never survive it." I don't make eye contact with him, and it makes admitting my private concerns easier.

"Look at me," he demands.

I direct my gaze to him without hesitation. He releases his grip on my arms and brings them down, pressing my palms against his naked chest. His skin is warm and tanned; his muscles bulge and ripple when he moves or speaks. He is intoxicating. I couldn't dream up a more beautiful man. He holds my hands in place against his chest as our eyes stay locked on each other.

"Nothing is going to happen. I won't let anything or anyone ruin this. You have no reason to worry. I won't let you lose anymore. Do you believe me?"

I do believe him. I know it's completely stupid, but fuck if there isn't a little tug in my chest telling me that I believe him. I nod.

"Say it, Josephine," he says firmly.

"I believe you."

He takes a deep breath and resumes his position beside me. "That's good."

"Can we eat now? I really want my burger before I have to get back to my place."

His grip tightens on me. "We can eat, but you're staying with me."

The way he said that has the clearest damn tone of finality I've ever heard. I can't just stay at his place all the time. I have to check my mail and pay my bills and wash laundry and other shit that normal people do at home.

"I don't have a choice. I have to...feed my fish." What? What the hell? Why am I lying about owning a fish? What's so hard about telling him hell no I have to go home because I have shit to do? I groan internally at my lie and lack of ability to sever myself from him. Fuck my life.

"Oh. You have fish?" He sounds skeptical. He's no idiot; he knows I don't own a damn fish, or dog or cat or anything else that requires food or love and attention.

"Yep. One of those cheap goldfish in the glass bowl."

He rolls me to face him and I wince a little on the inside; I know he can tell I'm full of shit. "What's his name?"

My eyes dart around as I scramble for a name. Shit. Shit. Shit. "Oh. Um. I just call him Fish." I shrug and pretend to pick at my nails. This is a mess. I'm no liar and apparently I should stay that way because I flat out suck at lying to Damon. I glance over and see a smirk play across his mouth.

"Okay, fine. I'll go with you." He releases me and rocks up out of the bed.

I watch his phenomenal naked ass as he makes his way toward the closet. Shit. He can't come with me. He'll want to know where the damn fish is. He won't accept no for an answer. I'll make it work; I can do this. I slide off his bed and join him in the closet. He glances at me as I walk in and start digging through my newly acquired collection of panties. I grab a lacey blue thong and slip it on. Damn, these feel nice. Damon walks over to me and stands right up against my ass as I work on choosing a bra. His hands reach around to cup my breasts and he rolls each of my puckered nipples between his forefinger and thumb. I close my eyes and let my head rest back on his chest.

His lips brush against my ear. "You're a shitty liar, baby."

I gasp as he punctuates his statement with a rough pinch of both my nipples. His chest shakes with laughter.

Jerk. I scoff at him and his hands fall from my breasts. He is full-out laughing now.

"Hey! Shut the hell up!" I put on a bra and turn to face him. His hand clutches his defined abs as he laughs uproariously. I perch my hands on my hips and scowl. "Are you done yet?" I snap.

He keeps laughing his awesome ass off. "A fish? I mean really? Baby, you have to know you are a shit liar. Damn, that was funny." He calms and catches his breath, stepping towards me with extended arms.

I'm not hugging him. Asshole. I bat him away and continue getting dressed.

"Oh c'mon, don't pout. It's fine. I get it. You need to go over to your place, but I want you to stay with me as much as possible."

"Fine," I huff.

"Besides, you need to stay with me tonight. I have a surprise for you bright and early in the morning."

I spin around to face him. He's gorgeous in just boxer briefs. "Tomorrow is Sunday, what could we possibly be doing in the morning?"

"Did you miss the surprise part, Baby?"

I roll my eyes. He's chipper as hell since I agreed to date him and I guess being chipper also means he's a smart ass. "Fine, whatever. Let's go. I have bills to pay and mail to check and I'm sure my trash can smells just splendid." I pull on a cotton cap sleeve top and jeans and spin in the full length mirror. Damn, my ass looks nice in these. I have to agree with Brian. Gay men apparently do have a serious sense of fashion.

Damon smacks my ass; no doubt he's thinking the same thing I am. "Need to give Brian a raise," he mumbles to himself. I snicker inwardly. He likes my ass. Total ass man. "C'mon baby. Quicker I get you there the quicker I get you back here. Let's go."

I smile and take his hand. I don't particularly enjoy the idea of going back to my shithole, but I have to. I won't be there long. I know he wants me here tonight and honestly, I do, too. I'm in deep already. Who wouldn't be, though? He's Mr. Fan-fucking-tastic. Any woman would be crazy about him. I'm no different.

I slide the key into the lock and open the door, only to be greeted by the disgusting smell of the leftover tuna salad I tossed out two days ago. "Ah, fuck! Tuna!" I run for the trashcan and cinch up the drawstring in a hurry, yanking out the half-full trash bag and hurling it out onto the front stoop. I'll carry the sour shit to the dumpster on our way out.

"Oh shit, open some windows, will ya?" Damon strides through my small shithole, opening windows as he goes.

"Geez, that's disgusting. Is there a dead Fish in the can or what?" I see him choke back a laugh at my expense and I glare at him.

"Har-har, very funny," I say flatly. I move through my place, making quick work of tidying up. I catch Damon watching me at every turn. I grab my mail and toss out most of it, since all I usually get is junk. I slit open my utility bill and nearly fall over when Damon whirls me around and snatches the pile of bills from my hand. "Hey! That's private!" I grab at the stack of letters, but he holds them out of reach. "What are you doing? Give them back!" Damnit! This is embarrassing as hell. He better not open them all. He'll see how far behind I am on my phone and electric bill and then I'll die of mortification.

He flips open the folded utility statement. Kill me now. I can feel my pride wither and fucking die at my feet. I turn and walk to my crappy futon couch. I flop down and my shoulders slump in defeat. I can hear him shuffling through my mail and I just want to crawl into a hole and die. I'm behind on just about everything, but my last two paychecks went into the garbage. I literally ripped them up and tossed them in the can. I knew Sutton didn't have the money to pay me, and the store is really my passion, too, so I figured if he isn't getting a dime, I shouldn't either. It was a sacrifice I made in hopes of buying more time to maybe save the store. I fell behind on everything in the process. It's all so screwed up.

He rounds my futon and sits beside me. I cross my arms on my knees and lean forward to hide my face in my lap. His big hand goes to my back and rubs small circles between my shoulders.

"What else are you behind on?"

I groan into my lap, but know that he won't let it lie. "A couple things," I say into my lap and it comes out sounding all muffled.

"The store?"

He apparently knows me well already. I've never been this transparent to anyone else. This openness and emotional shit is so far outside of my comfort zone.

"Yes," I admit reluctantly. "Sutton hasn't taken a dime recently because the store can't really afford it. I knew he didn't have the money, so I haven't cashed my last two paychecks."

"You aren't going to worry about any of this anymore, understand?"

I bolt up from my beaten down position. "What? You aren't paying my delinquent bills, Damon! I do have some pride."

His serious eyes and tightened jaw tell me I'm about

to battle this, too. Damnit! I can't win anything with him.

"So do I, and my woman worrying about money when I have an ass-ton of it isn't something I can be proud of. I'm taking care of your finances. End of discussion."

And there it is. Battle lost. Great.

"Okay." I can't even look him in the eye. This is a new low for me. No one has ever paid my bills. Failure feels like complete shit.

"Hey, don't you dare feel ashamed. What you did, forfeiting your money for Sutton, is admirable. Most people are too selfish to do such a thing. You're looking out for Sutton and the store. You're an amazing woman, whether you realize it or not."

Oh please, not again. Tears. Again. What's my problem? My lip quivers and I can feel them coming. "I just never wanted to see the store close. I tried really hard. I did." I wipe away the tears as they spill onto my face. I try to look away from Damon, but he won't allow it. His hand grips my chin and forces me to look at him, tears and all. Great. I have less pride and dignity by the minute.

"We're going to get things on track, starting tomorrow. Don't worry about it anymore."

I wipe my face and take a cleansing breath. I lean over to him and kiss him with all I have. I want him to know how grateful I am for him. I don't know how I got so lucky and I'm damn skeptical of it, but I'm happy to have him nonetheless. I may not be able to be proud of my life, but I'm damn proud to say that, for once, I have something to call my own. I have something I feel I can trust. I have Damon. Being his is something I can be proud of, and I am.

Chapter Thirteen

Appetizer

By the time we finish taking care of things at my place, it's dinner time. On the way back to his place, I offer to cook and he's happy for me to get back in his kitchen. I guess he likes my poor man cheeseburger casserole.

"We have to stop by the store. I need some ingredients that you don't have. I already looked."

"Okay, what store?" he asks in the most genuine way that I almost feel bad for laughing.

I look at him and a snort escapes me as I try to swallow down my urge to laugh. He seriously doesn't know shit about grocery shopping, does he? "The grocery store, Damon. You know, where they keep all the food," I quip.

He averts his eyes from the road for a split second to glare at me. It only furthers my amusement.

"You don't buy your own groceries do you?"

He looks over with that same damned sheepish look that gets me every time.

"Aw, you don't. My big, handsome lover-man doesn't know how to grocery shop, does he?" I say in a ridiculous baby voice.

"I absolutely know how to purchase groceries."

"Mhmm, sure you do. Just pull into the next grocery store you see...Big Man." I laugh under my breath again.

"Yeah, I'm going to show you just how big I am when we get back, smart mouth."

My stomach flips. I mean, actually flutters with excitement at his threat. I know he'll make good on it and I'm eager to get what I need from the store and get out!

"Promises, promises."

He turns into a supermarket parking lot and finds a spot. Once he opens my door and I step out his hand lands hard on my ass cheek and I yelp, right there in the parking lot.

"Keep teasing me, baby, and you won't be able to walk tomorrow."

Oh hell. Stomach flutters kick into overdrive and I flirt with the idea of encouraging him. He slips my hand into his and laces our fingers together. It feels nice, like we've done this for a million years and he's part of my identity. He's right when he says that seeing each other feels like breathing. It feels like breathing and living and all things good and right in the world; it feels like a damn dream and I dread waking up.

I stroll through the aisles with him in tow and grab the things I will need to make our dinner.

"What are we having?" he asks, tossing miscellaneous items in the shopping cart. He must feel like a kid in a candy shop.

"Chicken cordon bleu. My dad use to make it, but he never got a chance to teach me how, so I taught myself. I try to duplicate his recipe as best as I can. I think I have it pretty close."

"Oh."

Oh? Seriously? No back flips for gourmet cordon bleu? Damn. I guess my man likes to slum with his women and his food. I smile to myself over my private jab and keep walking through the store. Once we get all the things we need and check out, Damon gets us back to the penthouse so I can make dinner.

I fiddle around in the kitchen with all the gadgets and gizmos and cookware. His kitchen is really a dream; I could cook in here every day. "Hey, can I cook in here every day?" I muse aloud.

"Will you be here every day?"

Oh shit. Awkward. Does he want me here every day? I don't want to crowd either one of us.

"Because if it were up to me…" Damon rounds the island in the middle of the kitchen and stalks toward me with trouble written on his handsome face. "I'd keep you here all the time. Whether as my woman or my prisoner, it wouldn't matter. I'd still keep you. Right. Here." He jabs a finger down on the countertop and my eyebrows rocket up my forehead. He wouldn't! Wait. He probably would.

"You would, wouldn't you?"

A naughty smile eases onto his lips and grabs me about the waist, hoisting me up onto the counter. "You're learning fast, Baby."

I love hearing that slip off his tongue. "I love that," I whisper breathily, his fingers lightly grazing the inside of my thigh. My body responds to his touch quickly, and I feel the warmth of my arousal for him slicken my flesh.

"You love what?"

I know he's teasing me, but I'm fresh clay in his hands when his masterful touch is working my body. "When you call me Baby." My eyes roll back as his fingertips explore higher up my thigh, close to the junction between my legs. I inhale sharply when his hands cup behind both my knees and jerk me wider to accommodate his hips.

"Say it again."

I can feel his warm breath on my cheek and my body hums in response to his touch, to his voice, to his scent. I am completely at his mercy and I love it. "I love it when you call me Baby," I repeat.

His fingers skate to my thrumming center and slip beneath the surface of my shorts. "I can feel how much you like it." His thumb begins rubbing small, light circles across my clit and I moan as I lay my head forward on his muscular shoulder. "Tell me why you like it when I call you Baby."

I can't think, I can only feel. I smell him and I feel him. It's euphoric. The speed of his rubbing increases and my heart pounds in my chest. "Ah...I just...like it," I sputter.

His movements slow and I feel robbed.

"Uh-uh. Tell me."

Damnit! He's going to torture me until I tell him. "I-I don't know! I just like it."

His movements slow even further and I want to cry and slap him all at the same time.

"Tell me, Josephine," he growls in my ear.

"Because it makes me feel like I'm really yours!" I whine.

"Don't forget it, either," he rumbles as he shoves me

back to lie across the island. My back hits the granite surface with a thud. I don't even know how, but before I know it, my shorts and panties are missing in action, and Damon's awe-inspiring mouth is on my neglected pussy.

"Oh my, oh, Damon," I moan. My head rolls from side to side and his sinful tongue slides in and out, up and down. I've never come so fast. I feel my stomach tighten. My cheeks feel like they are on fire. My extremities are buzzing with a tingling sensation that travels throughout my entire body. "Ah! Damon!" I scream his name and see spots. I convulse right on the countertop. I shudder and shake as pure pleasure rolls through me.

Damon stands upright from his crouched position between my thighs, a naughty as hell grin on his face.

"Don't even fucking brag, guy!"

"Just say it one time. Come on, Baby," he purrs and it does the trick. I'm pathetic.

"It makes me feel like I'm really yours."

"Whose?" he taunts.

"Yours," I mumble.

"One more time. Whose?" He puts a finger behind his ear to mock being hard of hearing.

"Yeah, fuck off, Big Man."

He chuckles then presses his full lips to mine. I barely kiss him and he growls at my rebellion. "You had better kiss me, woman."

"No. It isn't fair how you manipulate me." I pout like a petulant child and smack on my best phony sad face.

"Come on, woman. Stop pouting and make me dinner. Just as you are."

"Thought you just had dinner," I toss out like a Battle of Wits Champion. He winks and my smartass tendencies evaporate into thin air. Fuck. He's so good at this game. I sigh heavily and wipe down the counter where he had his...appetizer. I get back to work making our dinner, naked from the waist down. I finish cooking, plate our food, and demand to wear my panties while I eat. Eating a hot plate of food while my bottom half is unclothed is just...hazardous. Damon saw it my way when I mentioned the ramifications of a burned vagina.

I cut into my plate of cordon bleu and pop in the first mouthful. It's to die for, just like my father used to make. Damon takes his first bite and chews slowly. I hope he likes it.

"This is amazing. You're a fantastic cook."

His compliment has me beaming like a teenage girl with a crush.

"I really wish I could have met your parents." He looks down at his plate and rolls the stem of his fork between his finger and thumb, making the tines twirl.

"I wish you could have, too," I admit. I do. I wish they could have met this gorgeous man that's setting up shop so easily in my heart. I wish we could have those damn family dinners every Sunday that most people dread. I would kill to have family card night, where we get together to gamble with fake money. I wish I wasn't so fucked up, then maybe I'd allow myself to have a husband and children... I shut off my stupid run-away thoughts when I feel a lump form in my throat. Damn emotions have been way out of control lately. The rest of dinner passes without us saying much of anything. I have a feeling the emotional shit involving family is a no fly zone for both of us.

"Dinner was outstanding. Thank you."

I smile as his superfluous compliment slides past my ears and goes straight to my heart, giving me a warm feeling that I'm beginning to like. A lot. I smile down at the sink of dishes I'm loading into the dishwasher. "You're welcome. Thank you for letting me cook in a real kitchen. I like it."

"Baby, you are the only woman who has ever made a meal in here, and if I have it my way, you'll be the last."

I freeze in place and look at him with wide eyes. "What?"

He makes his way around the counter and comes to

a stop close to my side. "Nothing. Let me take you to bed." He takes the dirty dish from my hand and closes the dishwasher, wrapping his arm around my waist. His hand rests on my hip and we climb the stairs in silence.

What did he just say? The only one? What do I say to that? Do I want to be the only woman who ever makes a meal in that kitchen? My heart pounds in my chest. I feel like I'm losing it a little.

"Don't overthink, Josephine. I didn't mean to scare you."

I draw in a deep breath of relief. My head tells me this is weird and moving entirely too fast; we just met, after all. He just hinted at me living here...or something. But, my heart is happy as hell. I'm so confused with myself. I need to sleep. Sleep should help me clear my head. Without saying a word, he leads us into the bathroom and turns on the carwash-sized shower.

"You have a complicated shower," I say as I strip off my clothes and let him pull me into the glass enclosure. He positions us beneath the warm spray and I lean my head against his chest; I could very well fall asleep just like this.

"Tired?"

"Tired. Satisfied. Full. Completely sexed up. I guess I could use some sleep."

He holds me to his chest as his hands reach for the

shower gel. He squeezes some into his hands and lathers it. He spreads the soap over my tired body; I take in the scent of his body wash and the feel of his hands on me. His soapy hand glides between my thighs and gently cleans me. I wince a little from the sore feeling our library sex earned me.

"Sore?"

"A little," I admit.

He makes a tsk-tsk noise under his breath. "Looks like I may need to be more careful with my woman."

"Maybe. Maybe not."

He looks at me with tender eyes that consume me on the spot. "I'll make that decision."

I give my hair a half-ass wash while I watch him lather shampoo through his own messy hair. His warm eyes stay on me, and watch as I rinse, then condition, then rinse my hair. We step out of the shower and towel off. I skip to the closet in a hurry to get some clothes on; I am cold after stepping out of the steamy shower.

Damon sweeps up behind me. "If you're cold, baby, let me warm you." His lips land on my shoulder and he guides us, naked and damp, to the bed. He pulls back the comforter and we climb in. My back meets his chest. He wraps his bare body around mine and the heat between us warms me in no time at all. The goosebumps go away and

160

the chattering of my teeth ceases. I breathe deep and snuggle closer into him. My eyelids become leaden and I feel sleep taking me over.

"I love this," I mumble hazily.

His arms tighten around me and his lips kiss the rim of my ear. "I hope so," he whispers and I relax into him further.

Chapter Fourteen

Lessons in Lady-Hood

"Wake up, beautiful."

"Uh-uh. Go away," I whine into the pillow. Why is he waking me up this early on a Sunday? The surprise! I bolt upward in the bed. I catch sight of him in dress pants and a button down shirt rolled up at the sleeves. His hair is styled in his signature dark mass of sloppiness, that no other man could pull off so flawlessly. I notice his clean shaven face and I grumble under my breath. "You shaved."

He grins, no doubt amused with my mood. "Come on. We have a busy morning. Lots of decisions to make, so let's go, woman, or I'm going to tie you up and spank that beautiful ass of yours."

"I don't know. It's tempting," I confess aloud.

His head shakes back and forth in disapproval. "If

you make us late for this meeting, I promise, Josephine, you're going to be a lot sorer than you already are."

Oh damn, he has a way of making me hot in exactly two seconds flat. "Okay, fine. What are we doing, anyway?" I roll out of his lush bed and stagger on stiff legs to his closet. I can feel him following me. I walk to the rack of clothes and flick through each hanger.

"It's a surprise," he says simply.

Great, a surprise. With Damon, it could be anything. I sigh and pull a sleeveless, pale yellow summer dress over my head. Stooping to my new collection of heels, I search for another pair of wedges. Damon notices.

"You need to learn how to walk in heels. You're my woman. We'll be going to parties and fundraisers all over town, and you'll be expected to wear heels. Now, put these on." He bends over and snatches up a pair of heels that make my insides shudder.

I look back at him and revive a long lost communication tool, my innocently pleading smile. I used it on Papa with great success. Now, I try it on Damon.

"Nope. Put them on."

"I'll slip and fall. Most girls learn how to walk in heels as teenagers. I never got those lessons." Okay, I know. Low blow, tossing out the dead parents card, but I really don't want to wear these.

His jaw tightens and he's clearly losing patience with me. "You're going to learn now. Put. Them. On," he grinds out through clenched teeth.

I snatch them from him with as much reluctance and disdain as I can muster. "Fine!" I snap, sitting on the floor without concern for lady-like manners, and shove one foot then the other into the strappy heels. I'll admit, they do look nice. I turn my feet from side to side and stand. Oh. Oh. I kind of feel like a total asswipe.

He quirks up an eyebrow and crosses his arms over his chest. "I take it they're not as bad as you thought."

I give a coy smile for the first time in my entire screwed up life. I made a big deal over nothing. These don't hurt and my balance is fine. Who in the hell told me high heels require a degree in lady-hood? "I feel kind of dumb," I mumble quietly. "They aren't bad at all. They're gorgeous and pretty comfortable."

Damon smiles triumphantly and I scoff internally at his brazen arrogance.

"Don't rub it in, Big Man!"

He shakes his head as he chuckles and pulls me in to hug him. He kisses my forehead and I close my eyes, breathing in his scent. It's soapy and a little spicy. I like it.

"Come on. Finish getting ready so we can eat and get to the surprise."

I scurry off to the bathroom to comb out my hair then apply my makeup in a dash. I can't help but notice that I took more care while putting on my makeup. Impressing Damon seems to be a priority these days. It's absurd and unlike me, but everything that I've been doing the past few days is unlike me. I glance at myself in the mirror before traipsing off to meet my Big Man at the front door.

"What are we doing here? The store's closed on Sundays." I look at Damon's handsome profile as he parks in front of the store.

"Exactly. Let's go." He smacks my thigh and hops out of his pickup.

I still find it odd that this type of man drives a pickup truck. Whatever. He opens my door and grabs me around the waist to lift me out of the big truck. He sets me carefully on my feet and, despite my nervousness, I seem to be fine in the heels. Go fucking figure, that Josephine Geroux can wear heels just fine. He clasps my hand and we walk, hand in hand, into the store.

"Who—what—" My jaw hangs wide open as I look around me. I watch a half a dozen men toting out the whole damn store through the back door. I don't know what the hell to think.

"It's in your hands now. Everything is being renovated and updated. You'll need to order inventory and speak with the decorator."

"Wha—I..."

Damon grins and pats me on the back.

I am speechless. I can hardly believe what I'm seeing. I've begged Sutton for years to figure out a way for us to renovate the store. It needs everything updated in the worst way. Our flooring is shitty, our ceiling is shitty, our furniture is shitty, our shelving; everything.

"We get new stuff?" I whisper as I lean in towards him.

"Yes."

I have to get out of here. I can't do this. I do an about-face in my heels, as if I've done it a million times before, and make a beeline for the door, barreling through it. My lip quivers and I could choke on the lump in my throat.

"Josephine!" Damon shouts behind me.

I feel him following me; it takes him no time to catch up with me as I rush down the sidewalk away from the store. I don't understand why in the hell he would do this. The store isn't some lucrative business venture or something. I'm shocked and grateful but there has to be a catch. Nothing this perfect just happens.

"Hey! If you want the old stuff, I'll have it all put back."

I shake my head no and keep fighting back tears. I hate fucking crying. I've only done it once a year for as long as I can remember, but since I met Damon, I've been crying every five minutes. When did I turn into such a fucking baby?

"Hey!" His big paw grips my arm and halts my getaway. "Talk to me," he demands.

The crease between his brows is deep and I suddenly feel like a jackass. Again. Damnit. I should be kissing his face off and showering him with my eternal gratitude, but instead, I've made him think I don't like it.

"How did you do this? Those men? It's a Sunday."

He releases my elbow and puts his hands on his hips when he sees I'm not going to run off. "This crew works for me all the time. They're getting paid overtime, trust me."

"I-this is too good to be true. *You're* too good to be true," I mutter.

His thumb and index finger lift my chin to look at him. "You're wrong, baby. I'm just doing what I want to, for you; to make you happy. So, you aren't losing the store;

I bought it so you can manage it. If you and Sutton can work out something, then he can stay on the payroll, too. And as for me and being good to you? I just want you to want and need me like I want and need you."

"What if I can't...make it work?"

"The store, or us?"

"Both," I admit. "We *just* met."

His amber eyes are luminescent in the sunlight, and they take on a look I have yet to see, a look of peace. I am fully and irrevocably enthralled by him. His thumb brushes across my chin softly, making one tender pass after another, and I start to relax under his touch.

"You aren't trying to buy me or hold the store over my head?"

"No. The bookstore is your passion, and I have faith that your ideas to bring in more business are great ones. As for us? I know we just me, but I feel like I've known you forever. I know we can work, because failing isn't an option."

"How are you so damn confident all the time?"

His hand falls away from my chin. I step into his space and wrap my arms around his middle. His arms encase me and I feel like I can breathe past the lump in my throat.

"I'm only confident when I know I'm right, and I'm

right about you."

"You're the best thing that's ever happened in my shitty life."

His arms tighten almost painfully and I feel his heart beat faster. I peek through my lashes at him and he looks like he may be ill. Oh shit, I've given the only boyfriend I've ever had the urge to vomit.

"Are you going to be sick?" I ask as I peel myself from his grip.

He shakes his head. "No, no I'm fine. You just scared me when you took off. I thought I upset you." He laces our fingers together and tugs me forward. "Come on, the store is waiting!"

Damon leans in and kisses me sweetly, then strides back of the chaos that is the bookstore, where a gruff-looking man is standing with a few other workers. "Excuse me one minute, I have to talk to the project manager."

"Holy shit, Jo," mumble to myself, looking around. The store looks huge with nothing in it. I have so many great ideas to vamp up the place and make it more appealing to the younger generation of readers. I'll admit, I'm still damn shocked over all of this, but over the moon happy. I love this store. Damon was right when he said the way to my heart would be through this place, because right now, I downright love that man for what he has done! I could spend the rest of my life trying to express my gratitude, though I fear I'd fall short. There's simply no way to thank him enough for accepting me and my shitty little world. I still don't get why the hell he is so taken with me, but, at this point, I don't care to try and rationalize it. He's the first good thing that has happened to me in a very, very, long time and damnit, I intend on indulging in this happiness. There's no telling how long it will last, anyway. The thought of us ending makes me want to curl up and hide, but I just have to set those worries aside. At least, for now.

Chapter Fifteen

Grams

Damon's been pretty quiet since we left the store. I feel awful for not being more vocal about how much I appreciate what he's done. Damn, I want him to know; I need him to know. That spot in my chest that gets warm and gooey when he does certain things isn't warm and gooey right now. Now it aches a little and I don't like it; I feel like I upset him. He's closed up on me and I have to fix it.

He said that on Sundays he visits his grandmother at the retirement home, so I reluctantly agreed to come with him. I'm nervous to meet his grandmother. I've never been anyone's girlfriend, so meeting the family is extra unnerving. He told me that she's really wonderful, but I can't help feeling like a ball of nerves.

He pulls us into the parking lot of a nice-looking old

folks' home and parks, rounding the truck to get me. He swings open my door and I crook my finger at him to come closer. He steps forward and I grab a fist full of his shirt, tugging him to me. I cup his angular jaw in my hands and lean in, pressing my lips hard against his, trying to convey what I feel.

"Thank you," I murmur against his lips.

One big hand travels up my neck and around my nape to tangle into my hair. He groans into my mouth and deepens the kiss, his lips drawing mine deeper. His tongue slips over my moistened lips and into my mouth. I welcome his demanding kiss, moaning and savoring the taste of him. He pulls away and I am left wanting.

"Do we have to visit Granny?" I whine like a child.

He laughs and lifts me from the truck. "It's Grams. Just Grams."

"Yeah, yeah, whatever." I smooth out my dress down my thighs and ass. He extends his arm to me and I take his hand. Deep breath, Jo; you'll be okay.

"Grams?"

We enter a room that would be better classified as a suite. This is the fanciest damn old folks' home I've ever seen. I haven't seen any, in truth, but this looks more like a five-star hotel than a place for old people to wither up. There are two fair-sized windows on the far wall with floral curtains held open to allow in natural light. Photo frames are propped on every surface. I glance at each one as we walk further into her suite. They appear to all be of Damon, some girl, and another man. Who are these people?

A frail looking older woman lies in the medical-grade bed. She's thin, with soft, white hair, cut short, and there's a vase of pink roses on her side table. I feel like running away now. I don't want to be here, she looks like death is a day away.

"Grams?" Damon calls softly, which I assume is so she doesn't startle.

She sits up and her eyes crack open; I can see now that this woman is nowhere near death! Her body looks like it's failing, but there's light in her eyes; she looks especially young in the eyes. They open wide in a crystal blue sparkle as she takes in the sight of Damon.

"Boy, get your rear over here and hug Grammy!"

"Grammy, huh?" I murmur.

Her eyes land on me and I feel like panicking. Her brows prompt an introduction, and on cue, my Big Man obliges.

"Grams, this is my girlfriend, Josephine Geroux. Josephine, this is my grandmother, Bernice Cole."

I extend my hand to her and shake her delicate,

boney hand. She looks to Damon and scoffs.

"Don't you repeat that awful name. Bernice! Can you believe my parents did that to me?"

Her radiant blue gaze lands on me and I swear to God, I'm smitten. This woman is like a senior version of me. I can see it. The minute I saw her eyes pop open, I felt it. She's feisty and I love it. I feel at home already. It's strange, but I'm grateful that I feel comfortable. I laugh in response to her remark about her name.

"You're right, it's a shit name." I admit.

Her grin spreads wide and her oversized dentures make me laugh harder. "I like this girl, Damon. Where did you find her?"

His smile is like heaven. He watches Grams and I hit it off like old girlfriends, and his mood changes drastically. "A bookstore. She was wrestling with a shoplifter."

He's exaggerating and I screw up my face in response. Drama king.

"Well?" Grams looks to me expectantly.

I raise my brows and look around in confusion. "What?" I question.

"Did you kick his thieving ass?"

I clutch my gut and lean forward in a fit of laughter. Damon follows suit with a low rumbling belly laugh. I sigh and wipe the tears from the corners of my eyes.

"He's lying to you; I only chased the asshole from the store. I got the book back, though," I say proudly.

"Well, good!"

I'm positively mad over this woman. I can see why Damon has a tolerance for my bullshit. His Grams is my far older twin. I feel a million times better about being the girlfriend meeting the family. I think I like this Sunday routine, I could hang out with Grams all day.

"Hey, could I maybe swing by to visit you tomorrow? I can make you some lunch and bring it with me?" My mouth moves of its own volition and the words escape before I think better of it. What the hell has gotten into me?

Then her face lights up and I don't regret my offer.

"It's a date, but only if you bring me a bag of those candy peanuts. You know, the big, fluffy, orange candy peanuts. This grandson of mine doesn't bring me a damned thing." She sticks her tongue out at him and folds her boney hands in her lap.

I smile wide. "I'll tell you what. I will bring you a whole damned box of them if you give me all the goods on the Big Man here." I jab my thumb out, motioning towards Damon and he grunts.

"Uh-uh. Hell no. No plotting between you two."

The rest of our visit with Grams goes by entirely too fast for my liking and I actually frown when he says we have to leave her to it. We say our goodbyes and I promise Grams that I'll see her tomorrow. Damon and I walk hand in hand to his truck.

"Was it as bad as you thought?"

"No," I admit reluctantly.

"So you mean I've been right twice today?"

"Yes," I mumble.

He heads towards his penthouse and I relax into my seat, preparing myself for his caveman ego stroking. He's been right twice in a row; I overreacted both times and felt like a giant ass.

"So what do I get for being right?"

I look over at him like he has lost his damned mind and see his crooked smile. My pride is no match for that damn smile. Or his honey eyes, or his sheepish look, and especially that extraordinary cock of his... It would seem that I am at his complete mercy pretty much all the time, and I can't say I mind a damn bit. I'm crazy over him. I can't deny it, not even to myself.

"It's a surprise." He smiles even brighter and the desire to crawl across the console and onto his lap nags at me.

"Don't tease me, woman."

"I'm not teasing you, baby. You deserve a lot after what you did today."

He glances over to me and his eyes are warm and tender. I want nothing more than to express my gratitude in the best way I know how. Sex. Long, hot, steamy, sensual sex. I plan on doing just that.

Chapter Sixteen

Two Parts

We walk hand and hand into the lobby of the Damon's building, making our way directly to the elevator, but Howard stops us.

"Boss?"

Damon stops and turns to Howard, who motions him over. Damon drags me to the security desk. "What's going on, Howard?"

The middle-aged man looks apprehensively at me and I feel like I should give them some privacy. I don't necessarily need or want to know what he has to say. I pull away gently, but Damon's grip tightens so I still.

"Uh, well, Edward came by earlier."

Damon jaw clenches and ticks. Who is Edward and why does his coming here piss Damon off?

"Boss, he was hammered again. Made a big scene.

Took me half an hour to talk him into leaving."

Damon nods tightly. "Thank you, Howard. I'll take care of it."

Fucking great, his mood is back to quiet and tense. I need to find out who this Edward guy is, but I'll wait until the opportunity presents itself; now is not the time. Right now, I'm going to work doubly hard to bring back happy Damon, because, though he's hot as hell, pissed off Damon has to go. We step into the elevator and he punches in the code with extra vigor. I know I shouldn't even bother, but I can't help it.

"Are you okay?" I ask while my thumb strokes along his hand reassuringly. He glances over to me and the anger in his eyes frightens me. I'm scared of very little. I've seen and done my fair share of screwed up shit, but the kind of anger I see in those eyes is the kind that makes a man kill someone. It scares me.

"I'm fine." His answer is short and total bullshit, but I choose to let it fly.

The elevator comes to a gliding stop and the doors slide open. He strides into the foyer with me in tow.

"I need to make a phone call. I'll be in my office. Make yourself at home." He leans forward and gives me a chaste kiss on the lips, turning and stalking through the big penthouse to his office.

I stand alone in his wide-open living space. It's cold and uninviting. I don't like all this modern shit. I head towards his kitchen and nose through all the cabinets. What to make for dinner? Hmm. A loud crashing noise emanates from down the hall and I freeze in place. What the hell was that? I slip off my heels and toss them beside the kitchen island, padding quietly towards the noise. I hear muffled yelling. I continue down a wide corridor. The yelling guides me to the end of the hallway, where I see a cracked door. I step up to the door and peep through.

"I told you last time was it! I told you I wouldn't do this anymore!" Damon barks into the phone. Holy shit, he's intimidating when he's mad. His fist pounds down on the solid wood desk. "Who the fuck do you think you are, coming to my home?!"

He's practically roaring now, and my heart pounds in my chest. My brain is screaming at me to move, to run away, but my body is frozen in place.

"Yeah, well the next time I see you anywhere near my home, I swear I will fucking kill you myself. You won't have to worry about his crew getting to you because I'll beat them to it. I think I should have dibs anyway, you sorry son-of-a-bitch!" He slams the phone into its cradle and runs his shaking hands through his hair.

Poor Damon. That had to be that Edward guy. My

hand moves involuntarily and pushes the office door open. His heads snaps to where I am standing and we hold each other's gaze for a long moment. My Big Man is shaking and rattled. I don't know who this Edward is, but I fucking hate him already. I walk to where he is standing behind his desk. I have an instinctive desire to comfort him; it's reflexive and seems to have come from nowhere.

His big frame plops down heavily into his desk chair. "I don't want to talk about it," he states with finality. His voice is slightly hoarse from shouting.

I hike my dress up so I can straddle him and ease across his lap. Even though my heart is pounding, I want nothing more than to calm him down. I want to fix whatever the problem is. I want to make it better. It's absurd, but it is what it is. I lean forward and softly kiss the edge of his jaw, wrap my arms around his neck, and hold myself to him tightly. The closeness of our bodies seems to mollify the tense atmosphere, and his arms come around my waist and hold me to him.

"I don't want to scare you, and that's what I did," he says softly.

I run my fingers through his thick dark hair and lean back enough to look him in the eye. "I'm not scared of you."

Relief washes over his face and it chips even more

crap away from my hardened heart; a clear pang of sympathy reverberates through my chest. I lean in and kiss his lips with unbridled intensity. His hands slide up my back to tangle in my hair. He flicks his wrist and wraps my mass of wavy hair around his balled fist. Our kiss breaks when his fist tugs my hair, causing my head to tilt back. His mouth feasts at my neck, warm moist lips kissing me passionately. His fist tightens in my hair, making me whimper. He releases me and I seize the opportunity to do what I want. I grind once against his erection, then slide off his lap. I kiss his lips once more before getting to my knees before him. He looks like a man in charge, and I'm both turned on and alarmed at the realization that I like him above me. In charge. In control.

I push my alarm aside for dissection at a later time. My fingers go to his belt and deftly unbuckle, unbutton and unzip his trousers to free his flawless cock. It springs up and juts outward towards me in invitation. I close my hand around his considerable girth and stroke from the base back up to the tip. I repeat the movement and watching him closely. His eyes are hooded, but remain on me. I inch closer to his chair and give him one last glance before I glide my tongue from root to tip. My tongue swirls around the wide tip of his cock and he groans. I feel his body tense, then relax. I take him into my mouth and seal my lips around his silky smooth length. A guttural groan vibrates through him as I draw him deep into my mouth, to the back of my throat, then forward again. I back him out of my mouth and kiss the tip, collecting the lone drop of moisture. I lick the residue from my lips and savor the taste of him. The scent and taste of him is a heady combination that has my stomach clenching deliciously. I take him deep into my throat for pass after pass. I stroke the base of his cock as my lips draw tight around him; my tongue flicks occasionally against the tip and massages the sensitive zone on the underside of his shaft.

His hand skates across my cheek to my head where his fingers lace through my locks. I work him fervently until I feel him lengthen and tense in my mouth, then gentle my movement and swallow down the surge of his warm release. His hips buck forward as he spills into my mouth. I lap at his length and lick him clean.

I've never been so turned on in my life. I'm frantic to have him in me. He reads my body language and springs from his seat, lifting me to him. I wrap my legs around his waist and hold on for dear life as he rockets up the staircase. The bedroom door gets his foot again and he lays me reverently on his bed. He sheds his clothes in a flash and makes quick work of removing my dress, bra and panties. He kneels between my legs and runs two fingers down the seam of my pussy. He bites his lip and his eyes roll back in ecstasy.

"Fuck, you're wet baby," he purrs seductively.

My body writhes in response to his touch on my skin and his voice in my ears. He plunges his two fingers into his mouth and sucks them clean. He leans across the bed to reach his nightstand, withdraws a condom and rips it open. I am compelled, possessed, by my need to feel him. I want him on me and in me. It breaks my own rules, but I don't want a damn thing between us. I still his hands and take the condom from him.

"Nothing between us," I say breathily.

His head tilts back and he brings his attention back to me; the pure lust burning in his eyes has me emotional and wanton beneath him.

"Please," I beg.

He leans forward and cages my trembling body with his intimidating frame. "You're sure?" he asks hesitantly.

I nod my head, affirming what I want. Him, plain and simple, bare and mine.

He breathes in heavily as he positions the wide head at my entrance. It's the first touch we share intimate skin on intimate skin, and it lights my body on fire. He stays in place, poised to penetrate me. What is he waiting for? He's shaking and I can tell he's restraining himself; he's holding back.

"You have to tell me if I'm hurting you."

I nod.

"No, say it. Promise you'll tell me."

"I promise." The moment I say what he wants to hear, he surges forward, driving his erection deep. I gasp and claw at his back.

"Oh fuck, baby, you're the first. I've never gone bare."

Knowing that we are each other's first at least in some capacity makes my heart swell. "Me too."

He groans his appreciation in my ear and his lips draw my lobe into his mouth. He bites down lightly and my body tenses in response. I tighten even more around his cock and he loses all control. He grips my hips and hauls me into him with force. My legs are pushed upward to rest on his shoulders. The very tip of him burrows deeper into me. I suck in air through gritted teeth. His hold on me is nearly crippling, but I'm not in pain. Pure lust rages in his eyes. His cock withdraws and thrusts forward over and over with ferocity that would rival any wild animal.

"Ah, Damon."

A bead of sweat rolls from his hairline down his forehead and finally drips from his nose to land on my sternum. "I need you," he pants.

My hands fist the pillows beside my head. The tingling sensation that flows through my veins inundates my senses. All I can see is him. All I can smell is him. All I can hear is him. All I can taste is him. All I can feel is him. I feel so completely his and the sensation is like none I have ever felt. I want to be his. I want him to need me like he's said.

"You have me," I moan as he continues deep, penetrating thrust after thrust. I can feel every unique ridge and vein of his erection as it slips past the outer rim of my slick opening.

"Again," he demands through gritted teeth. His honey eyes blaze as he gazes down at me. Sweat blooms from my pores and makes the friction between us non-existent. Our bodies slip against each other with complete fluidity. We fit. We look the part. We are two parts made whole.

"You have me," I repeat with as much sincerity as the moment allows. My body comes alive in a new way and hums with my impending orgasm. Every muscle tightens and tingles and I focus my eyes on his.

We watch each other as our respective orgasms unfurl and consume us. His hips buck as he releases deep within me. Warmth fills me and my channel spasms around his cock, drawing out his climax. Our bodies shudder and lurch repeatedly, blissfully. He pushes my legs from his shoulders and collapses in a sweaty, exhausted heap. His chest rises and falls rapidly while he works at catching his breath. I push my fingers through his sodden hair. My own exhaustion overtakes me; my eyes close and I feel completely sated in a way I've never known.

"We're meant to be this way," he whispers.

Chapter Seventeen

Special

"Baby?"

Kisses rain down on my cheeks, nose, chin, forehead, and neck, making me stir from slumber, "Uh," I grunt incoherently.

Damon chuckles under his breath. "Dinnertime, let's go."

I guess I should probably get my oversexed ass out of bed and make Big Man something to eat. If fucking like that is what I get from him, then I will gladly load him up with plenty of carbohydrates and protein. He's a bull of a man, he needs to eat. I push myself up and pry my eyes open. Damon looks gorgeous in bare feet, jersey shorts, and a white undershirt. I purr my approval. He shakes his head and smiles that crooked smile; the one that makes me impossibly weak for him.

"I may have created a monster."

"Perhaps," I muse as I walk past him, completely naked. I feel his eyes follow me and I turn to face him as I walk into his bathroom. "Mind if I piss in peace?"

His sheepish look falls into place right on cue and I'm pleased with myself. He's just so damn cute when he looks utterly embarrassed.

"I'm kidding. I don't have to pee. You showered without me?"

He continues to follow me into the gargantuan bathroom. "You were out cold and it's the only time that dirty ass mouth of yours is shut, so I figured I'd better savor the moment while I could."

I spin around to face my dark-haired bull of a man. His arms are folded over his broad chest. The smirk on his mouth is all the evidence I need to see that he is in a playful mood. It's a world away from the furious man I encountered in his office earlier.

"Smartass, huh? Well, that's too bad. I was planning on something special when we took a shower. Oh well, maybe next time."

"Oh, bullshit, woman! I told you not to tease me." He strides towards me and tosses my naked body up over his shoulder and walks right into the shower, fully-clothed. He flips on the taps and cold water pelts my ass and back.

"Put me down!" I squeal in protest.

"You've been a bad girl, you need to be punished," he growls comically, trying his best to look malicious.

"No! It's cold!" I slap his ass through the sopping wet shorts, but his big paw slaps me back, and soon it's an adolescent, ass-slapping free-for-all. "Ouch! Put me down!"

"Are you going to tease me anymore?" he sputters between deep laughs, positively shaking with mirth.

"Okay! Okay! No more teasing! I promise."

Satisfied with my white-flag-surrender, he slides me down the front of his body. His arm snakes around me to adjust the water temperature. Warmth pelts my skin as he holds me close. I tuck my fingers into the waist of his shorts and tug them down. Water streams down his body and drips from his face. I lean in and greedily collect the water from his stubbly chin, then tug the hem of his soaked shirt up and over his head. Our lips clash together. He drinks from me as I drink from him. I pull his full bottom lip between my teeth and his groan sends a pulse of electricity racing through my body. He cups my ass and in one easy movement lifts me to him. My back crashes against the tiled wall as he impales me with his hard cock.

"How's this for special, Baby?" he growls, taking a fistful of my hair in his hand and tugging so hard that my head gracelessly thuds against the wall. He has me pinned, his body holding me in place easily as his cock works me hard and fast, driving hard and deep, over and over.

I moan and his mouth covers mine, silencing me. His tongue delves deep while stealing my breath. My heart pounds out of control under his ministrations. He breaks away from my lips and rams into me harder.

"Who do you belong to?" he demands in a shout.

It's so hot and I feel like I may come with just his words. My tender pussy tightens exquisitely.

"Say it!" he bellows.

"You!" I whimper weakly.

"Again!"

"You! I belong to you!" I cry out breathlessly.

He thrusts hard once, twice, three, four more times and freezes, then his body lurches and stills repeatedly. My own pleasure crests and crashes down over me. I roll my eyes back and arch into him. My sensitive, hardened nipples press against his pectoral and I delight in the sensation. His warmth spills into me and his cock twitches as we ride out our climactic pleasure. He holds me in place against the tile wall until my breathing has returned to normal. When he eases out of me, a small zap of pain radiates through my womb. I reflexively wince and suck in a breath of air.

"Did I hurt you?" he whispers, one big hand cupping my jaw.

The concern in his voice is clear. I feel...valued; cherished. And dare I say, loved. I know there's no possible way he could love me. We are as fresh as a couple could be. I still don't know his favorite color, movie, or drink. I've never had the love of anyone except my parents, and I don't even remember it as clearly as I used to. Memories have faded with time, but this sensation feels familiar and I swear it feels like love. I say nothing as I look up into his warm, honey-colored eyes.

His other hand moves to my face, thumbs brushing reverently across my cheeks. He rests his forehead against mine and closes his eyes, breathing deeply. In this moment, something is communicated between the two of us. It's indescribable and disarming, yet somehow puts me completely at ease. We hold each other under the water, until his stomach rumbles loudly and we both dissolve into laughter; the moment broken.

"Come on, Big Man. I'll make us some dinner."

He lightly smacks my ass when I turn away from him to wash my hair and body. Yeah, he's definitely an ass man. We finish up in the shower and towel off before heading down to the kitchen. I zip through the kitchen like a woman on speed. Working in this space is so nice. I enjoy cooking, but I've never had the proper kitchen or tools to really flex my culinary muscles.

He steps up behind me and plants a tender kiss on my neck. "What would you like to drink?" he mumbles against my skin.

"Mmm, do you have any wine?"

He steps away and opens his monstrous refrigerator. "I don't, sorry. I don't really drink much so there's no alcohol in the house."

"Maybe we should go get some. I don't know about you, but I could use a drink." I talk to the cutting board as I season our steaks.

"I'd prefer if we didn't."

His tone has changed and I stop what I'm doing to face him. "Why?" My curiosity wins out over my better judgment and I want to know.

He moves about the kitchen, collecting utensils and dishes to set the table. His muscle capped shoulders shrug nonchalantly. "My father's a drunk, has been all my life. I just don't care for the shit."

Note to self, alcohol is a no-go. I suppose it's really no big deal, I don't drink very often anyway. I like the occasional beer or glass of wine, but it's pretty sporadic. Not to mention expensive.

"Oh." It's the only thing I can come up with. What

the hell is my problem? Should I hug him? No. I would hate that shit. I decide to just leave it alone and change the subject. "So, what do I have to do tomorrow at the store?"

"That's easy. I've already worked out the details for tomorrow with Dave, my Project Manager. The decorator will be here at nine o'clock tomorrow morning to go over some things with you."

I set the steaks to broil and drain the potatoes. "Wait, I'm meeting the decorator here?" I dump the steaming hot potatoes into a mixing bowl with the butter, milk, and garlic and smash them up as I carry on with our conversation.

"Yes. The store is now a construction zone and I don't want you getting hurt or hanging out around a crew of horny construction workers." His explanation sounds reasonable, except for the horny crew part. He sounds a tad jealous, but I don't even want to broach that subject with him right now.

I finish preparing our meal and we eat and carry on light conversation, mostly about the store. As I'm clearing the dishes and contemplating suggesting something that couples do like watching a movie, Damon's phone rings. He glances down to the screen and his jaw clenches and ticks.

"I have to take this," he says flatly and stalks to his

office.

I talk myself out of eavesdropping and focus on cleaning up the kitchen. Whoever's on the phone has to do with this Edward person, I'm sure of it. I kill time and wander into the library, choose a book from one of the many shelves at random, and pad to his bedroom. I crack open the book and the spine creaks, moaning its protest. This book has never been opened. Its unmarred spine speaks volumes to me. My eyes lazily scan the first page before sleep wins out and I give up on reading.

Chapter Eighteen

Hi, Mom

I wake up feeling like someone ran me over with a bus and I can't blame this on rough sex. I'm getting sick. Fuck my life. I roll over and, through cracked lids, spot a note on the bedside table. I reach across and snatch it up. Scrawled in shitty, man-bull writing is a short and sweet message.

You're right next to me and yet I miss you. —D

I look around for signs of Damon, but find none. I dress quickly in a pair of Damon's pajama pants and a white tee and drag my aching body down his stairs. I can hear movement from the kitchen. I walk in to find Damon staring at the oven like it's the mystery of all mysteries.

"What are you doing?" I force out sounding very similar to an eighty-year-old smoker.

He whips around like I've screamed bloody murder.

"You sound awful!" He rushes to me and lays his hand across my cheek. "You have a fever. You have to get back in bed."

"What the hell were you staring at the oven for?"

He looks back over his shoulder and looks sheepish again. Damn him. "Ah, well, I was thinking maybe I could make you breakfast, but I'm afraid I'm not as proficient in here as you are."

I laugh in spite of my sore throat. "I like how you dressed that up to sound far better than what it is."

"And what is it?"

"What you should have said was, 'I can't cook for a damn, so breakfast is out.'"

He laughs and turns me by the shoulders to direct me back to the stairs. The doorbell chimes, halting both of us. I thought guests had to be let in through security?

"That'll be Carrie." He releases my shoulders and jogs over to the fancy front door, opening it and stepping aside.

Something deep within me rears back and surges forward in a hurry. Oh, hell no. Carry is a fucking life-like Barbie, complete with ridiculous spray tan. She smiles coyly at Damon.

"Come on in." He motions his arm forward and she struts past him with an exaggerated sway in her hips.

Bitch! She doesn't even notice me standing near the staircase in my too big pajamas with no bra. My hair is a mussed mess and I feel awful. Meanwhile, this bitch looks like she's trying to win a damned beauty pageant.

"When I got your message, I was glad to squeeze you into my schedule. So, what are we working on, Damon?" she asks, with as much innuendo as possible.

I have an impulse to tackle this tangerine Barbie and strangle her. "Ahem." I clear my sore throat and draw their attention to me.

"Carry, I'd like you to meet my girlfriend, Josephine. You'll actually be working with her on the project. She's in charge of all things regarding the store, so you'll need to answer to her."

His insinuation of answering to me makes me beam on the inside. This man is after my heart in a fierce way and damnit, he's succeeding. I smile warmly at him as he walks away from the spray tan poster child.

He comes right up to me and rests his hand on my cheek again. "Baby, you have a fever. This is going to have to wait, okay?" He leans forward and kisses my scorching forehead.

I catch a glimpse of Miss Spray Tan behind him and she looks as if she just caught a whiff of something putrid. Her over-glossed pink lips crinkle up and look like an overused and abused vagina. Gross! I just can't resist. "You really ought to stop making that face. You know, wrinkles and all,"

She jacks up her face even more and I choke down a laugh. Damon turns from my side to face her and she instantly plasters on a phony grin.

"We'll have to reschedule, Carry. Josephine isn't feeling well. I'm sure she'll call for another appointment when she's up to it." Yeah, right, how about never, skank?

"Okay, that's fine. I'll let my secretary know that you'll be calling to reschedule. Bye." She turns in her patent leather heels and matching cream-colored pencil skirt and leaves the penthouse.

The moment the front door closes, he sweeps me into his arms like a baby and totes me to bed, tucking me in and smoothing my hair back with immense care. He sits beside me with a cocky smirk on his face. I sigh dramatically and roll my eyes. I know what's coming.

"Baby, are you jealous?"

The intonation of the last word makes my anger level rise again. "I'm no more jealous than you, Mister 'stay away from the crew.'" I imitate a ridiculous, macho voice and he points a stern finger at me.

"Hey, I'm only looking out for your safety! A nail could go through your foot or something."

I laugh a little too hard at his absurd excuse and my sore throat burns more as a result. "Ouch," I croak, clutching at my neck.

"Okay, enough joking around. I'm working from home today so I can take care of you. I'll get you some medicine. You rest now." He leans in and kisses me, despite my potential contagiousness, and it leaves me with that vaguely familiar feeling of being cared for. Cherished. Loved. He rises from the bed and disappears from the room. "He leans in and kisses me, despite my potential contagiousness, and it leaves me with that vaguely familiar feeling of being cared for. Cherished. Loved. He rises from the bed and disappears from the room. He returns with a glass of water in one hand, and ibuprofen in the palm of his   other   hand. "Take these. Drink all of the water if you can." He holds the medicine and water out to me. I pop the pills in my mouth,   then   gulp   down   the   water. "Rest now." My eyes do as I'm told. I rest."

I sleep deeply until I feel a slippery tongue glide across my cheek and I furrow my brows. Why the hell is he licking me?

"Pssst!"

"Hmm?"

"Wake up," he whispers and then licks my cheek

again. Gross!

I push my heavy eyes open and scream, scrambling backward and smacking up against the headboard. "What in the hell is that?" I shout, then instantly regret my response; yelling did my throat no favors.

"Don't freak out," Damon admonishes. "It's just a puppy. He likes you, he was kissing your face." He pulls the silver and gray fur ball into his chest and rubs him behind his little scruffy ears.

"You got a dog?" I know I sound incredulous. This ultra-modern penthouse would look just great with puppy shit on the floors. I can't believe he got a damn dog. "I thought you were going out to get medicine for my poor, sick self?"

"No, I got him for you. Well, I guess he got me. He's an orphan," Damon explains. Why'd he have to use the word 'orphan'? Now I feel like the puppy and I are old pals. It's ridiculous. I raise an eyebrow to prompt and explanation and he complies.

"One of the guys on the crew found him by the dumpster at the store. It was just him, no tags or anything. Dave's wife is a vet, so he called her down and she checked the little guy out. She said he's some type of Schnauzer mix." He produces a brown paper bag from behind his back. "See, I got breakfast and the medicine, too. Throat lozenges, tea, vitamin C…"

"Thank you," I rasped, grabbing the bag. "But Damon, I can't have a puppy at my apartment."

He shrugs in response to my objection. "He can stay here."

I pop a throat lozenge and narrow my eyes at him; I see what the hell he is playing at. "If I agree to take this…thing, and he has to stay here, it stands to reason that I'd have to stay here as well."

A victorious grin spreads across his handsome face and I know I am screwed. He holds up the scruffy-looking thing and manipulates his tiny paws in a praying gesture. "Oh, please be my new mommy. Won't you adopt me? Aren't I cute, mommy?"

I try and fail to stifle my laughter. "You know you sound completely stupid, right?"

Damon sets the puppy in my lap and I reluctantly stroke his fur. He's so soft, and he's kind of cute. Actually, he's really cute. I lift him up to my face for a closer look and find myself gazing into his tiny, chocolate-brown eyes.

"How old is he?"

"Dave's wife said he's probably between eight and ten weeks old."

I roll out my lip. I can't believe he's so young and so alone. I feel awful for the little man. He deserves a home and I know I have to take him. I don't know the first damn thing about taking care of a dog, but I guess I can wing it.

"Hemingway," I say to the little furball in my hands. His tiny ears perk up in response. I set him down in my lap and pet his tiny head.

"What?"

"It's his name. Hemingway."

Damon scoffs and I shoot him a hateful look. Asshole!

"What's wrong with Hemingway?"

He shakes his head from side to side. "You can call him Hemingway, but I'm calling him Hemi. Like the engine." He's adamant, I can tell. It has to be a man thing.

"Fine." I look down to Hemingway and scratch behind his ears. "Daddy says he's calling you Hemi, in spite of your obvious intellect and sophistication."

Hemingway lets out a high-pitched little bark and I nearly drop him. Damon clutches his gut and lets out a deep belly laugh.

"He's a puppy, he's not going to hurt you."

I shoot another death glare in his direction and cuddle Hemingway to my chest. He tilts his little head up and licks my cheek again. I melt into a puddle of female hormones and animal instinct.

"So, do I get any points for bringing you a puppy?

Women like puppies."

I look at him and wonder for a brief moment if his story is all bullshit. I bet he went and bought this dog for some insanely high price from one of those fancy dog breeders. But I look into little Hemingway's brown eyes and recognize the loneliness and apprehensiveness of an orphan; he has to be what Damon says. Poor little guy. He gets points. Loads of points. He rescued Hemingway from who knows what and I guess I have someone to...love?

"Points." I affirm and lean forward to kiss him. "Loads and loads of points."

Damon's face turns even more victorious and I swear his chest couldn't poke out any further. Geez. Men and their pride. It's the downfall of society.

"Oh, shoot. I told your Grams that I'd be there today with circus peanuts!" I cradle Hemingway to my chest and slide out of bed.

"You're sick," Damon protests as he follows me to the bathroom.

"I feel much better," I lie. I shove a plush bath towel into the sink basin and carefully set Hemingway in it. He curls up and plops down. I smile, feeling a little proud of my ingenuity.

"Are you sure?" He reaches out to check my temperature with his hand and I bat him away.

"I'm fine, really. You brought me all the essentials, I'll be 100 percent in no time. You go get some work done, whatever that might be. I'll be back here once I'm done visiting your Grams. I promised her." I make sure to sound pleading on that last bit. I know he wouldn't want to upset Grams.

He sighs and I know I've won the battle of wills.

Chapter Nineteen

Makes Sense

I say goodbye to Damon and send him into his office to get some work done, then scurry from the penthouse with Hemingway tucked into the crook of my elbow and a travel mug of tea. We ride the elevator down to the first floor and I locate Damon's Beamer, which I really wish I wasn't about to drive. I tried to argue with him, but he shoved the keys at me and did the clenched jaw thing. I click the locks with the fancy key fob and slip across the supple leather seat.

"Sweet," I mutter to myself. I situate Hemingway in my lap and start the car. We set out towards the store to find circus peanut candy for Grams. I think I've seen that stuff at the convenience store near my apartment.

"Stay here," I say to the fur ball and lightly tap his nose. I hurry inside the store and luck out, a full shelf of the sugary stuff. I open my bag when the cashier gives me my total, dig out my wallet, and nearly piss myself. A wad of hundred dollar bills are shoved haphazardly into my wallet.

"Ahem, ma'am?"

I snap out of my shocked daze and pay for the candy, hurrying back to Hemingway and the Beamer. I don't waste any time; with a flick of my thumb, I'm dialing Damon. He answers on the first ring.

"Hello?"

"You shoved thousands of dollars into my purse!" I bemoan. I sound like a dumbass. Who complains to their boyfriend about being so damn generous?

"Do I need to remind you of our conversation about being proud?"

I groan. I should've known that no amount of protesting would make a difference. My wealthy boyfriend isn't going to let me struggle, and I'm grateful for that, don't get me wrong. There's no doubt about how much I appreciate him and all he has already done for me, but I don't like feeling like a charity case or a burden. It's a complex, I guess.

"No. Thank you," I reply. Stupid, stupid, stupid. He's just being nice.

"You're welcome. You may want to go to the pet

supply store for Hemi. He'll need all that puppy stuff."

I look down at Hemingway, curled snugly up in my lap, and realize that I haven't the slightest clue what the hell a puppy requires, besides food, water, and a place to shit. "Okay, I'll take care of it. See you later."

"Bye, baby."

Twenty minutes later, I pull the Beamer into a parking space and carefully stuff Hemingway into my bag. The pliable little puppy doesn't even wake when I move him from lap to bag.

"Grams?" I tap on her open suite door and am happy to see she isn't napping. She cranes her neck to peek over at the door and her face lights up, beaming smile reminding me of her grandson's.

"Josephine! Did you bring the goods?" she asks in a low, discrete tone.

I shake my head at the old woman's antics and dangle the plastic shopping bag at her.

She takes it from my hand and smiles wide as she counts the bags of candy I brought. "Oh, honey, you've made my month!" she coos.

I'm proud to have pleased her. It seems stupid to be happy about bringing her some candy, but part of me really wants her to like me. I guess it's probably the same part of me that knows I could easily fall for Damon in a major way.

"So, how are you feeling today?"

She waves me off as she stuffs a circus peanut into her mouth. "I'm fine. I ran a couple miles this morning and that always makes me feel extra spry." She winks at me, holding out the bag of candy, I can't help but fall head over heels in love with the old woman. She has an amazing personality that I can really relate to. I want to tell her as much.

"I bet you never take any shit off anyone, do you?" I remark, swiping a peanut from her hand.

"Well, am I white, made of paper and come rolled up on a cardboard tube?" she asks, straight-faced as could be.

"No."

"Then no. If I took shit off anyone, I guess I'd be better off named Toilet Paper."

I nearly choke on my circus peanut and the old hag cackles her ass off at me. "Touche. Touche, Grams."

We continue to eat candy and I open my bag every minute or so to check on Hemingway. He's fast asleep, curled up in the darkness of my big bag. I like this little fur ball. He's easy to please.

"So who are these people in your picture frames?" I walk over to a frame sitting on a side table and lift it to show her.

"Oh, that would be Damon's half-sister, Elise. And just there in that silver frame is my son, Edward. And that brown frame next to that is Damon, at his high school graduation."

Edward. Edward. The guy who pissed off Damon last night. He said his dad is a drunk. Makes sense. I decide to press for information.

"So, I guess Damon and Edward don't get along very well?"

She makes a huffing noise under her breath. "They don't get along at all, honey. I love my son, but I'm not very proud of the things he's done. When Damon came along and his mama couldn't keep him, she gave him over to Edward. Now, Edward didn't want Damon either, but I sure as hell made that son of mine handle his responsibilities. I didn't raise him to do the things he's done, but I have tried to make wrong things right, as they come."

She hangs her head slightly when she talks about Damon's father and my chest aches for her. It's obvious that she's dealt with more than any one woman should. I feel the need to cheer her up and I think I know the trick.

"Hey, want to see what Damon got me?"

She nods and I reach into my bag and lift out

Hemingway. His gray fur is standing out in all directions and he squints against the light, then starts wiggling like mad when he sees Grams. She gasps and lights up when she sees the little fur ball, holding her hands out for the wriggling mass. I hand her the puppy and watch as she cuddles him and kisses the top of his little, apple-shaped head.

"Oh, that's just like Damon to use a puppy to gain your love and affection. The boy has animal instincts like no other. It's why he's so successful, you know," she observes, obviously proud of her grandson.

We visit for a while longer, then I decide I'd best get going. Despite popping what seems like the entire package of throat lozenges, I'm starting to feel gross again, I have no idea how often puppies eat or use the bathroom, and I still have to get to the pet store, then back to Damon's place. I say my goodbyes to Grams and promise to visit again soon.

"So, I don't suppose you could help your new mom out by cluing me in on what the hell I'm supposed to buy you? No? Okay, Hemingway. We'll figure it out together." I sit in the driver's seat, holding my fur ball up to my face. We gaze at each other, green eyes to brown, nose to snout. He just hangs there. I set him back in place in my lap and drive towards the pet mega store. It's the size of a supermarket and people drag their pets in to shop with them. I'm surprised to find myself a little excited to buy him some puppy things, whatever they may be. It makes me wonder if he's had anything at all. Puppy food in little puppy bowls, a bed to sleep in, a hand to stroke his fur... I look down at him and the place in my chest, where I assume my heart lays dormant, warms and aches for little Hemingway.

"Let's buy some shit," I say to the sleepy puppy as we exit the car. I walk into the pet store and, on an emotional impulse, buy with someone else's money. I fill two carts with shit that the dog may or may not even use. I think I bought one of everything. He now has everything from puppy vitamins in the shape of a doggie biscuit to a stroller. A damn stroller. I know I'm going to catch all kinds of shit for buying the doggie stroller, but what if I want to take him on a long excursion like the tag says? He may tire in Las Vegas heat. The stroller is useful. That's exactly what I'll tell Damon. I pay for my purchases with Damon's wad of hundred dollar bills and load up the Beamer.

"Now that we've done some damage, let's go see your new Daddy and show him all this shit. What do you say, Hemingway?"

He stares at me, then opens his puppy mouth wide

and yawns. I kiss his little head and put him in the passenger seat for our trip back to Damon's penthouse. I park in his reserved space and dial him from my cell phone.

"Hello, beautiful," my Big Man chirps into the phone.

"Hey, um, could you maybe come help me bring up these bags? I'm sitting in your car."

I hear him chuckle into the phone and I'm suddenly shy about my emotionally charged shopping spree.

"I'm on my way."

I hang up and gather an arm full of things, including little Hemingway.

"Wow. One dog needs all this?"

I turn to see my big, dark-haired man standing behind me. He's so handsome, I melt instantly. I step to him and lean in to kiss him. "I felt bad for him. I guess I bought a bunch of shit. Look at him, though!" I shove Hemingway at Damon.

He collects the puppy into his big hands and talks to him in a babbling baby voice. "Aw, da widdle man wooks wike he's sad," he blabs. Oh, God. I hope I don't look or sound that dumb when I talk to the dog.

"I bet he thinks you're the town idiot, talking to him like that. His name is Hemingway. He could be a literary genius like his namesake for all you know," I say, completely snarky.

"Yeah, you're right. I should kiss his furry little ass. Come on, I'll have the bags brought up." He tosses his arm across my shoulders and we stroll into the high rise like a real couple with a real puppy. It's a novel concept in my shitty life. I like it. A lot.

Chapter Twenty

Familiar Loss

"If you had read the instructions like I told you..."

"I don't need the instructions. It's a small dog stroller. It can't possibly be that difficult to put together. I think you bought a faulty one. We're missing a screw."

I hold the phone to my ear and scowl at his stubbornness. It rings and rings and Sutton doesn't pick up. It worries me. He always picks up for me. Why isn't he answering? My usually void and cold heart clenches hard in my chest and pounds out of control. "Something's wrong. I can feel it. I've got to go. I've got to check on him." I'm panicking.

Damon gets to his feet and grabs me by my shoulders. "Deep breath." His voice is demanding and comforting at the same time.

I close my eyes and inhale deeply through my nose

and out my mouth.

"Now, let's stop by his place and see if he's home. Come here." He pulls me into his arms and holds me tight.

It's soothing, but only marginally. I feel it in my gut, something's wrong. I kiss Hemingway and put him in his new crate.

"I'm sure he's fine. Maybe he's in the shower or something."

I wish he was right, but I know what I feel and what I feel is that something's off. "Just hurry, okay?"

He presses down on the pedal and we whiz through traffic to get to Sutton's house.

"Turn here. It's the third house on the right. See the gray four-door?"

"Got it."

Damon comes to a stop, but I'm already out of the car and running up to Sutton's door with my key in hand. He gave me a copy a few years ago, just in case of emergencies, and this feels like a fucking emergency. I jab the doorbell three times and immediately start banging on the door with my balled fist. Damon is at my side almost instantly.

"Captain! You home?"

I bang on the door three more times and jab the doorbell three more times. I hear a crash from inside the house and I move, lighting fast, to open the door. The key slides into the lock and the deadbolt releases. The door jams and Damon puts his shoulder through it, sending the door flying back to crash into the wall. I run into the house and skid to a halt on the old hard wood floor.

"Oh shit! Captain! Captain! Oh, no. What happened?" I skid across the floor on my knees, bending down to him. He is in an awkward position, lying on the floor in the living room. The crash I heard was the damn telephone. He's pulled it down from the end table. His face is contorted and something is very wrong.

"Oh, fuck. Call an ambulance!" I scream frantically to Damon. I hear him speaking to a dispatcher. I gather Sutton's shiny, bald head into my lap and wipe the spit from the corner of his mouth.

"Oh, please. Please. Hang tight. You're fine. You're going to be just fine, Captain. Don't worry. Help is coming. Just please hang in there," I plead with him. His glossy eyes roll about aimlessly and I know this is horrible, something bad has happened. I squeeze his hand and he doesn't respond.

Damon crouches down beside me and presses two fingers to Sutton's wrist and something alarming flashes, but I can't place it. I feel so out of control right now. I'm shaking, my adrenaline is pumping fast through my veins.

"Where are they?" I cry out, on the verge of tears.

"They're coming, Baby. They're coming."

The sound of sirens is a welcome thing. I hear them draw nearer until an ambulance and two police cruisers screech to a halt in front of the house. Two paramedics walk in with big, black duffle bags in hand.

"Sir, Ma'am, we're with the Fire Department. Please step back." They elbow their way in to help Sutton. They take his head from my lap and start saying a bunch of shit in paramedic code language.

I don't know what they're saying and it makes me angry. "What's going on? What the hell is wrong with him?" I scream at them.

They ignore me and keep working on him. Damon wraps me up in his arms and pulls me back. I feel like I'm watching everything from above. How did this happen? Why didn't I get here sooner?

The third paramedic turns to me, placing a comforting hand on my arm. "Ma'am, I need to ask you some questions so we can better help him."

At this point, the police and paramedics have blurred together and my brain feels hazy. He asks me a string of questions and I know the answer to about half of them. I don't know what the hell he last ate. I don't know if he has had any strange symptoms today. I haven't spoken with him since he called two days ago to tell me about the store. What if he's been lying here all this time? What if he's been waiting for me to check on him? Maybe that's why he was trying to get to the phone. I cup my hand over my mouth, completely mortified at the thought that he may have needed me and I was eating fucking circus peanuts and shopping. Tears well and the lump in my throat is crippling. I gasp for air, but the choppy, short gasps don't seem to make it past the lump. I see colorful spots and I feel myself sway and lean into Damon.

"Shit!" is all I hear Damon call out through the heartbeat I hear thrumming in my ears. It's dark.

"Baby, wake up," Damon says in a calm voice.

I jar awake, fully aware of what's going on. I hear the sirens ahead of us as we speed to the hospital right behind the ambulance they must have Sutton in.

"You passed out. You're okay, I've been with you the whole time. How are you feeling?"

I ignore his question with one of my own. "Is he okay? Did they say he would be okay?" I watch his profile from the passenger seat fall. Not good news.

"They think he may have had a stroke. He's showing symptoms consistent with a stroke."

I feel my adrenaline kick in anew as panic grips me all over again. I run my hands through my hair and stare blankly at the ambulance in front of us.

We park in the emergency lot and I run for the Emergency Room. Damon clutches my hand and we jog into the building.

"Stanley Sutton? He was just brought in by paramedics," I pant out.

"I'm sorry, ma'am, you'll need to be seated in the Waiting Room. Someone will come speak with you as soon as they can."

I pound my fist down on the nurse's desk and turn away. "Damnit!"

"Hey, take a deep breath, okay? You have to try to stay calm," Damon soothes, running his hands back and forth down my arms. "We don't know anything yet. He's in good hands here."

I let him lead me to a chair in the corner of the Waiting Room. He folds his large frame into the uncomfortable chair and pulls me into his lap. I cooperate, sitting across his legs and drawing mine up into his lap. I nuzzle my face into his neck and the tears and panic wash over me. An hour passes in what feels like ten. A doctor appears on the far side of the Waiting Room. The nurse who told us to wait speaks with him and points in my direction.

"Sutton?"

"Yeah, yeah. How is he?" I ask hurriedly.

"Are you family?"

"Yes, she's his granddaughter." Damon responds authoritatively, before I can even think to speak.

The doctor nods. "Okay. We have your grandfather stabilized and he's being moved up to the ICU on the third floor." He takes the empty seat directly in front of us and my heart drops. This isn't good. He glances at my left hand then back up to my face.

"Ms. Sutton, I'm afraid your grandfather has had a massive stroke that has caused significant brain damage. The scans show that he has considerable bleeding in his brain. We've done everything in our power to help him. Now we have to wait and see how he does in the next twenty-four hours. I'm sorry I don't have more promising news for you. You can go upstairs and sit with him. He is only semi-conscious and likely very confused. I'll be in to check on his status as often as possible." He reaches across and takes my hand in his and squeezes. "I'm so sorry, Ms. Sutton."

I stare at the doctor in a daze. I've heard what he

said, but nothing registers. A stroke? His brain is bleeding? How did that happen? I'm not even sure I know what exactly a stroke is. Fuck!

Damon lifts me from my seat and guides me to an elevator. "Josephine, look at me." He cups my face in his hands and forces me to look at him. "I'm here. I'm not going anywhere. I'll make sure you're okay."

The same flash of familiarity jolts through me. This entire nightmare has me reliving the accident; the sirens, the paramedics, the hospital, the doctors, the nurses. It's all stirring up the sheer terror from nearly two decades ago and I feel like I may falter beneath the weight of it all. I walk with Damon to the Nurses' Station. I must look like a zombie; my eyes are open, but they're locked in a vacant stare, looking at nothing in particular. I'm thinking clearly, but my eyes refuse to move or focus on anything. I stare blankly at the floor.

"Sutton?" Damon asks a nurse.

"Room 328."

Damon leads me away and my eyes remain locked onto the floor as we walk. We enter a room that's much dimmer than the hall. I hear the sound of machines, and it snaps me out of my daze. I look up to see Sutton lying very still in the hospital bed. He's hooked up to all kinds of shit. Wires lead to and from his body; I have no idea what they all do, but the sight of them sends a chill down my spine. It's bad. Really, really bad. Damon leads me to him and I nervously perch myself on his bedside. He stands beside me as I reach out and run the back of my hand across Sutton's weathered face. My throat tightens painfully. I gather his wrinkled, frail hand into mine and cover the top of it with my other hand. I'm careful not to tangle with his IV line.

"Captain, please," I croak out through my tears. "Please don't go. Not yet. Don't leave me." I shake my head and tears stream, uninhibited, down my cheeks.

He watches me hazily through heavy lids. I can tell he wants to say something, but he's just too weak. His skin is pale and lifeless. I feel panicked; I don't know how to handle this. I may have a screwed up, dysfunctional relationship with Sutton, but he's all I have. He's been like a parent to me and we may pretend to hate each other, but we have a special bond. I have him to thank that I'm off the streets. I came in and all but demanded a job and he gave me a shot. I used my pay from the store to buy the headstones that my parents deserved. I was able to eat decent food consistently for the first time since I was a little girl, before the accident. I managed to put a roof over my head and bought a real bed to sleep on. He took a chance on me and it's a debt that I can never repay. His hand squeezes mine just a bit as he closes his eyes. A crimson bead rolls from his nose and my sobbing turns uncontrollable. I know it's the last time I'll see his eyes open and I feel my heart break with an all too familiar sense of loss.

Damon pulls me to my feet. He hauls me into his chest and wraps his arms around me. In one easy swoop, he lifts me into his arms and I bury my wet face in his neck. He walks to the small sofa by the window and sits down, swings my legs across his lap and cradles me to him. Nurses burst in and soon the room fills with medical staff who works, in vain, to revive him.

"He isn't going to make it, is he?" I croak out through bone-wracking sobs.

"No, Baby, I don't think so."

I lean hard into Damon and drown in my own tears and sorrow. I've lost Sutton, my Captain.

Chapter Twenty-One

Dangerous Despair

Three weeks hasn't changed a thing. I should know this, of course, but somehow I was hoping Sutton's death wouldn't hurt nearly as much as my parent's death. I was naïve to think such a thing. He was a father figure to me for seven years. I saw him six, sometimes seven days a week. I ate most of my meals with him. He always respected me and never judged me. He could tell I was screwed up, but never pushed me to talk about it. I loved him for that, even if I didn't realize it. I nearly fell to pieces when I found out that he left me everything; his house, his car, the life insurance money...everything. I knew he had been estranged from his daughter and granddaughter for years, thanks to some bad blood between him and his ex-wife. I never asked for the details and he never shared; I was fine with that, but I never expected to be named as beneficiary in their place.

Sutton left me everything and three weeks have passed with me staring at the paperwork. I have the deed to his home, the title to his car, and a whole file folder stuffed to the brim with important documents I know nothing about; everything. I don't know what to do with it. I can't move into his house, but I don't feel right selling it. It's a nice house, but this place is Sutton's, not mine.

Damon has been incredible; my saving grace against the familiar, dangerous despair that's knocking at my door. His presence is the medicine that soothes my wounds. I've clung to him over the last few weeks and he's gladly carried the burden of a grieving, miserable girlfriend. I feel like he's all I have in this world, and while that sounds immensely daunting, he's more than enough. He's everything. He's it. He's the one. I know it like I know my own damn reflection. If ever two people were designed for one another, it's us. I've never believed in the whole love at first sight soulmate bullshit until now. Until him.

I've been in his bed the whole time. All work on the store halted with Sutton's death. Damon insisted that I not worry with the project, so I haven't. I thought about going to the store, but just thinking about it hurts in a way that steals the air from my lungs and makes me want to double over. I'm so fucked up.

"Baby?" Damon walks into the room with a glass of orange juice in his hand.

I hold Hemingway to me and roll from my side to face him. My easygoing pup doesn't mind in the slightest. "I love you, Hemingway." I bury my face in his soft fur and he licks my chin, giving me a whiff of his sweet puppy breath.

"Hey, beautiful."

I scoff at his compliment. I'm nowhere near beautiful right now. I'm pasty and sallow without a bit of makeup on; my sweatpants and camisole are dingy and my hair is limp and lifeless. I look like I've been in bed for a month. "Not beautiful."

"You're always beautiful to me and my opinion is the only one that counts."

I smile sweetly at my Big Man and wish like hell I wasn't so damn screwed up right now. "I'm sorry," I mumble as I absentmindedly stroke Hemingway's fuzzy coat. "I don't know what's wrong with me. I'm not being very fair to you."

The bed dips as Damon crawls in and scoots to my side. He lays on his side, fully dressed in his usual slacks and dress shirt. His warm honey eyes watch me closely and he's quick to brush away the two rogue tears that slide down my cheeks..

"Listen to me. You're the most important person in my life. You're hurting right now, and you need me. Nothing makes me happier than knowing you need me. It makes me feel important, and...l-loved."

He stammers out "the L word" and my heart stills, then swells with more love than I could ever express to him. It may be the emotional train wreck that Sutton's death has made me, or maybe this is just what falling for someone does to you. I've tried to solve this puzzle for a week solid. I met him and I started feeling, and crying a lot, and wanting, and smiling, and a whole host of shit that I never did before. I even have a sweet little puppy that I love and spoil to pieces.

He looks hopefully at me, his adorable, sheepish expression in place, making my emotions spiral out of control. More tears seep from the corners of my eyes and I can tell he's feeling nervous about mentioning "the L word."

"I've been thinking about it, and I want you to see a doctor. You're depressed. I've already set it up and you have an appointment tomorrow morning."

"I love you," I confess in a voice that matches his sheepish expression. It's small and weak, but no less powerful.

His eyes slowly slide closed and he exhales a deep

breath, as if he's been holding it. He leans in and cups my face with his big hands, pressing his lips tenderly to mine. He kisses me with passion and longing and a relief that is palpable. If a kiss could say what he feels, this one is screaming *I love you.*

"Again," he says softly, with his eyes still shut.

I'll do as he says. I'll repeat it. I could say it a million times and never tire of telling him. "I love you." That time my voice is more confident.

He draws in another deep breath, as if he is soaking up my confession, then slides across the bed and stands, his back to me. What in the world is he doing? I see him bow his head, unbutton his shirt, and slip it off. His pants meet his shirt on the floor and he turns to face me. His amber eyes have a new look in them, warm and intense and loving. I can look into those eyes and see the depths of what my Big Man is feeling. He remains silent, setting little Hemingway in his puppy bed on the floor. I peek over the side of the bed and see that the spoiled pup has plopped down and is right back asleep.

Damon crawls back into bed and kisses me chastely before tugging the camisole over my head and tossing it to the floor. His fingers slip into the waistband of my baggy sweatpants and free my legs. Since undergarments have become a nuisance, I stopped wearing both bra and panties to bed. I lay before him, completely bare. He scoops my legs up behind my knees and spreads me wide to him, his cheeks staining a light pink, hinting at his arousal. I know that mine mirror his, I can feel the subtle heat on my face. My body hums with anticipation as I watch him pull off the snug-fitting, gray boxer briefs. His erection springs free in all its glory and bobs heavily in my direction. My mouth waters to take him deep and have his taste on my tongue. His palms rest on my bent knees and he looks desperately deep into my eyes.

"Again," he orders.

I oblige the man I have fallen for so completely, "I love you."

He looks almost in pain as I profess my love for him and I watch his chest rise and fall with each deep breath he draws in. He's magnificent. He slides down on his stomach and gets comfortable between my thighs. His soft lips land on the sensitive inner part of my thigh, causing my legs to tremble, and his warm hands stroke down my legs soothing away the quivers as he goes. His lips travel up my leg and past my center to land on my stomach, just below my navel.

"Again," he mumbles with his lips pressed to my skin. His warm breath assails my skin and makes my core tingle and tighten.

"I love you."

He groans as I repeat myself again. His hands skim up my body and his face levels with mine, amber eyes digging into me. He holds my gaze for a long moment. The wide, heavy tip of his cocks butts against my slick opening. Pure heat has collected low in my stomach, waiting for him to take me. My legs drop wider as my body opens to accommodate his hips. He settles in between my thighs and brushes strands of loose hair from my forehead. He thrusts forward just enough to breach the tip past my wet lips. My eyes shut while I wait for him to make love to me for the first time.

"Again," he demands in a firm voice.

I can tell that it's taking everything he has to restrain himself.

"I l-love..." As I start to speak, he rams into me, stealing my breath and the words from my lips.

"Say it," he growls and stills, perfectly buried to the root.

"I love you, Damon. I love you more than anything in this world!"

A tear slips from the corner of my eye. He brushes it away with his thumb then threads his fingers with mine and stretches them out high above my head.

"I couldn't possibly love you any more than I

already do. Josephine, my heart resides with you forevermore."

He remembers the quote on the back of my mother's watch. The same quote my father said to my mother. My heart squeezes painfully and I swear I could die of contentment.

"Oh, Damon," I croak out as more tears escape my eyes.

"Don't cry, Baby." He moves his hips back, withdrawing himself to the very edge then easing forward, slow and deep. I feel the tip of him bump against the deepest parts of me. He leans down to bury his face in my hair, which is splayed gloriously out on the bed. His profession suddenly makes me feel like a goddess, and I turn my head to nuzzle his neck. His movements remain slow, steady, and deep. Tears still roll from my eyes as he makes slow, magnificent love to me. I prop my legs as high as I can manage, allowing him the deepest access. His speed increases fractionally and I know we're both on the verge of climax. He pants heavily in my ear and I arch into him as the building tsunami of pleasure prepares to inundate me.

"Ah, don't stop. Don't stop!"

His speed increases even further and one hand releases mine to grip my hip, his hand sensually tight and feather light at the same time. The momentum with which he pushes into me is all-consuming. Breathtaking, even. My toes curl, my core tightens, a momentous build of energy peaks and crashes down. My body spasms and bucks hard as my channel clenches hard around Damon's cock. He thrusts into me over and over then stills, his cock twitching and jerking. He spills his release into my depths and collapses, releasing my other hand sighing as I wrap my arms around him. I brush his back with the pads of my fingers and feel as his breathing slows and his heart rate returns to normal.

"Say you'll stay with me. No matter what." His muffled demand comes off as more of a request. Why would he say something like that in that way? There's no way I could leave, ever. I am completely and irrevocably his. No other man could hold a candle to the way I feel about Damon.

"I could never go back to life before you. You're all I want. You're all I need. I'm not going anywhere. Ever. You're stuck with me, handsome."

I can feel his lips turn up into a smile against my neck. He withdraws from me and remains resting half on me, half on the mattress.

"Even if it takes the rest of my life, I swear to you, I'll make you forget every bad thing that has ever happened to you. We'll make happy memories that will outweigh the sad ones ten-fold. I live to make you smile, Josephine."

"Well, I'd say you're off to a great start, Big Man." I thread his hair through my fingers and lightly tug.

"Good. That means this next part will be easier."

He props himself up on one elbow. The mischievous grin on his face speaks volumes and I slant my eyes at him suspiciously.

"Uh-oh."

He puts up a hand to postpone my pending rebellion. I may be in love with him and looking forward to spending my every waking moment with him, but I still refuse to take shit off of anyone. Like Grams says, "If that were the case, I'd be better off named Toilet Paper."

"I've decided that you're moving in with me. Officially. Your apartment is being packed as we speak."

He chances a look at me and I see the worry flicker in those honey eyes of his. Aw, hell. I can't leave him hanging like that. On the inside, I feel like someone just opened the drapery to my world and let in some light. I've been here for nearly a month, so I love the idea of officially living here. I can't imagine being anywhere else. On the outside, I must look panicky, because he's obviously worried about my reaction.

"Before you go and begin throwing a fit, you should realize a few things. This subject is simply non-negotiable." Damon holds up his hands, fingers popping up to tick off each one of his points. "I'm your boyfriend. I love you. I worry about you. I'm horny almost always, and you are too. I think you're going through a depression, and you need me. You haven't stayed at your place even once in a month. Then, there's Hemi. I wouldn't want to get into a nasty custody battle with you, Josephine, but don't test me." He winks after the last bit and I roll my eyes.

"Never! He loves me best!"

He clutches his chest dramatically, earning a laugh from me. "That's because you're the mom. Everyone knows the kids always love their mommies a little more. You spoil the shit out of him, too."

His accusation has me feigning being aghast. I absolutely spoil Hemingway, but that's my job. I love him too much to not spoil him.

"Fine. Since it is non-negotiable and all."

He beams a panty-obliterating smile at me and I'm sure I visibly wilt before him. If heaven exists, then I'm sure this must be it.

Chapter Twenty-Two

Skeletons

"Are you having any thoughts of harming yourself or others?"

I narrow my eyes at the schmuck sitting across from me. "No," I clip out. I'm not fucking suicidal. I'm grieving. That's it! I don't think I may hurt myself, but if he asks one more irritating question, I may contemplate bashing him over the head with that damn leather-bound notebook.

He watches me like the shrink he is and jots something down on the pad in his lap.

"You know, taking notes about me is really pissing me off. So save your fucking note taking for later. Okay?" I slap my palm down on the arm of my chair. This is ridiculous. I was all for the idea of seeing a doctor, but I didn't think it would be like this. He's agitating me. He's a nice-looking older man, but his lack of response to me is beyond frustrating. Is this what therapy is supposed to be like?

"Why does my note taking bother you?"

"I don't like the idea of you...just...talking shit about me in your little notebook. You don't even know me, so how could you write anything about me?"

He gives a clinical nod and continues writing. Jackass.

"Why would you have the impression that I think poorly of you? That I would write 'shit' about you?" He uses air quotes, which only perturbs me more. It's irrational. I'm aware of that, but damn he is getting under my skin.

"I don't know. Maybe because I'm dating a rich entrepreneur who paid you six months in advance to see me because I'm a fucked up, formerly homeless orphan with a host of skeletons just itching to jump out of the closet?"

"I take it you don't feel like you're on the same level as Mr. Cole?"

I look at him like he is the world's most dense person. "Um, what part of that comparison did you not get? Super rich entrepreneur. Homeless, unemployed, orphan." I hold out my hands like a scale and quirk up an eyebrow.

"Josephine, I don't believe Damon views you like that. So why do you define yourself in such a way? Why can't you say something else?"

Well, shit. I don't have an answer for that. "I don't know," I mutter and flick a piece of lint from my jeans. "I guess I've never thought of myself in another way."

"Okay, well right now, I want you to define yourself differently to me. I want you to introduce yourself to me and say all positive things about yourself."

"Right now?"

He nods and I see his stupid pen ready to jot.

"All right. Um. I guess I um, I work hard. I don't quit easily. I can take an ass kicking, verbal or physical, and keep going. I taught myself most everything, since I quit school when I was twelve. I'm really good with books, Sutton used to call me a walking card catalog." Thinking about it makes me smile, but sadness follows almost instantly. I'm still getting used to the fact that he isn't at the store waiting on me. It still hasn't sunk in that when I stop to get Chinese takeout, I won't be ordering his usual sweet and sour chicken.

"Let's talk about him a little."

I glance up at the old shrink and I'm compelled to talk. "I went to The Diner this morning for my usual breakfast routine and I swear on my life, I saw an older man walking through the parking lot who could be Sutton's twin. My heart stopped when I saw him. I know it can't be, I mean, I put him in the ground. Right beside my parents, actually. I was the last one to see him before they closed the casket. He looked peaceful. Like he was sleeping, you know? They closed it in front of me and wheeled him to the hole in the ground. Only four people came to his funeral. Me, Damon, Brian, out of respect for Damon I think, and one of his neighbors. That's it. No one cared that he died. It still makes me sad and pissed off. More people should fucking care! More people should fucking hurt! Not just me! I'm so tired of it just being me. It's not fair that it's always me!" I've rambled on and broken down into a sobbing, bone-wracking fit of emotion. The good doctor comes to me and squats down in front of me. He hands me a tissue and pats me on the back. He sets the tissue box in my lap and returns to his seat.

"Josephine, you're mourning. You're mad and that's normal. It's normal want to blame someone for the things that have happened. The first step I want you to work on is embracing the things that have hurt you. Stop fighting against all of it. Allow yourself to hurt. Allow yourself to cry as much and for as long as it takes until you get it all out. You can't go on suppressing all these things. You have a future waiting for you and I can see that you want to go for it, but you have to cut your ties with the past, young lady."

I nod and blot my eyes. "I know. I want to try. I really do. Damon deserves better. He's amazing and I love him. I'll try for him."

The doc gives me a half smile and checks his watch. Right on cue, our first session is over.

"Til' next week, Doc," I say, giving him a finger salute. "Thanks."

When I get to Damon's BMW, I rest my head against the steering wheel. I don't want to go back to the penthouse yet. It's a bloody wreck thanks to moving boxes full of my useless junk. I can think of someone to cheer me; my ticket in is a bag of circus peanut candy. Perfect.

After stopping by a gas station to get the goods for Grams, I hightail it to the retirement home. I adore that woman and honest to god, she's just what the doctor ordered right about now. She is wise and funny and smart. I could use the distraction of a nice, long visit with Grams. I pull into a parking space and shut off the car, stopping to fire off a text to let Damon know where I am.

Stopped to visit with Grams. Be back soon. Love you.

A text hits my inbox a minute later. I open it as I walk across the parking lot.

Again. :D

I smile a broad, face splitting smile and type out another text.

I. Love. You. ;)

Another text chimes as I make my way down the corridor to her suite.

Atta girl. I love you too. Kiss Grams for me.

I shove my phone into my bag, and round the corner and walk through her open door.

"Hey, Grams, I brought y—"I freeze in place when I see that she already has company. "Oh, I'm sorry. I can come back."

"No, you don't! Bring me that candy, girl!"

I give a tentative smile and continue into the room. An older man with glassy, bloodshot eyes and silvering blonde hair smiles a toothy grin from the chair beside Grams' bed. Who the HELL is he? I hand the candy over the Grams, who tears into the bag like an addict, and wait for an introduction.

"Josephine, this is my son, Edward. Eddie, this is Josephine, Damon's girlfriend."

His eyebrows arch up and he crosses his arms over his chest. "Ahh. So you're the mooching little whore who I'm supposed to stay away from."

"Who the fuck do you think you're talkin' to, you

drunk ass slob?" I fire back.

"Hey! Both of you, knock it the hell off!" Grams easily breaks up our squabble and we're resigned to dirty looks and eye rolls for the rest of my hour-long visit. So much for being cheered up.

"Mom, I'm off." Edward, that drunk piece of shit, leans over and gives Grams a half-assed hug.

Opportunity knocks.

"Yeah, I guess I had better take off, too. Damon is waiting." I lean in to kiss her on her wrinkled cheek and hug her.

I jog to catch up with Edward in the hall. "Hey!"

He stops and turns to face me.

"I don't know who the hell you think you are, but talk to me like that again and I'll jack that jaw of yours into next week!"

The next thing I know, his disgusting hand comes crashing into my face. This motherfucker just slapped me like he's lost his mind. Without thinking, my hand draws back and then my balled left fist lands squarely on his lousy, drunk mouth. He grunts and clutches his bloodied mouth.

"Don't you ever put your hands on me again," I grate out through teeth so tightly clenched they grind together. I turn and head for the exit. I glance at a nurse as

I leave, her eyes wide with shock. Damnit, I'm going to get banned from visiting and Damon's going to be pissed. Just what I need right now.

On the drive home, I tried to come up with a decent excuse for my pending ban from the retirement home, but came up with nothing. I bet they've already contacted him to tell him about my fist fight with his dad.

"Fan-fuckin'-tastc." I mumble to myself as I press in the code and the doors shut to take me directly to my doom. I'll just be honest and explain myself. It's the only play I've got so I'll just go with it. If he's pissed, I'll just grovel until he gets over it. Yep. It's a plan.

"I'm back!" I shout. No one comes. Where the hell are they? Hemingway usually comes slipping and sliding on his clumsy puppy feet to the foyer. "Hello?!" I walk down the hall towards Damon's office, slowing my steps when I hear talking. Who's here? I slip through the half-open door to his office and see Damon in the chair and Hemingway sitting on the desk, attentively looking at the computer screen.

"What about this one, Hemi? What do you think? Think she'll like it?"

Damon ruffles Hemi's furry little head before noticing me at his door. His jaw clenches and I know he's pissed. He sets Hemingway down on the floor and comes to me in a hurry. He grabs my hand from my side and drags me towards the bedroom. Ah, shit.. His hand grips my jaw and forces me to look in the mirror and I see why he's flipped out. My lip is busted and blood has dried just below my bottom lip. Damn. I didn't even feel it. Or taste the blood. Adrenaline is funny like that.

"Who busted your lip?" His chest is heaving up and down, his face has turned red and one fist is balled so tightly his knuckles have turned white.

"I got into it with your dad. He slapped me, so I punched him. He looks worse than me."

"Josephine, I am not impressed with your humor. Tell me what the fuck happened. Now."

"He was there with Grams, he called me a mooching whore. I stopped him in the hall to tell him not to run his mouth like that to me and he slapped me, so I landed a left. Busted his shit up good, if I do say so myself." I say the last bit with pride because it's true. His face bled a lot more than my measly little drop from a busted lip.

"I'll kill him. I swear to Christ, I'll bury that sorry piece of shit! He's ruined my life already, I won't let him mess with you!"

Chapter Twenty-Three

Answers

"You didn't have to clean it like a mortal wound, you know. That antiseptic really hurt!"

Damon turns his still-furious amber gaze on me and I decide that my mouth should probably stay shut until he cools down. I offer a weak smile, but wince when my busted lip cracks open. The wimpy display only fuels my Big Man's anger. He points a finger at me and I freeze in place.

"If you see him again, you leave. I don't care where you are. You leave and call me immediately. You don't go anywhere near that motherfucker. Do you understand me?"

His tone and urgency have me a little freaked out. I can handle a lush just like any other person, but something tells me he isn't the typical drunk asshole.

Something distinct in Damon's voice has me genuinely worried. He had a creepy, sinister grin on his face when I walked into that room. It wasn't the kind of grin that means anything good. I need some answers, but it's clear that they won't be coming from Damon. He is far too pissed and adamant about me keeping away from his father. I'll have to talk to Grams again.

"I'll steer clear of him, baby. Just calm down, okay?" I step into his arms and brush my palm over his sculpted cheekbone. "You don't have to worry about me. I'm a big girl." I smile, but it does nothing to coax him into a lighter mood.

"You don't understand, Josephine." He shakes his head and pulls me into his chest. His arms tighten around me and I can barely fill my lungs. He's freaked out. Something isn't right here.

"He ruins everything he touches. He sucks the life from everyone around him. He uses and hurts people, then throws them aside when they're of no use to him anymore. I would be completely destroyed if I ever lost you because of him. I'd never make it without you. I don't want to make it without you."

His words have me worried and deeper in love all at once. It seems that my poor Big Man is screwed up, like me. Maybe I should drag him to see the shrink. I laugh on the inside at the idea of Damon sitting in the chair I was in, talking to my new shrink about whatever. I can't picture him doing it.

"Have you ever been to a shrink?" I blurt the question before I have a chance to think it through.

"Yes. I've been seeing Dr. Versan for years." He releases me and starts putting away the first aid kit.

"Oh. I—he didn't say." Not giggling any more. Years? How screwed up is he?

"He isn't supposed to say anything. I told him not to. Besides, he is bound by patient confidentiality," he explains simply.

"When did you start seeing the old geezer?" I know I shouldn't push him, but I want to know, I have to know. I'm pretty screwed up and he knows what all my issues are with the exception of a couple, but I know next to nothing about his past. He never brings it up, and until now, I haven't cared much to push the subject.

"A long time ago. I was a teenager when I became his patient. Grams found him for me."

That's it? "Wh—"

"I don't want to talk about it right now, okay?"

"Hey." I reach for his arm and stop his tidying. "When and if you want to talk about it, I'm here and I'm not going anywhere."

"That's precisely why I don't want to talk about it."

What? I scrunch up my eyebrows, confused by what he just said.

"Now. Let's move on to more...pleasurable topics." His hand wanders up my cotton dress and goes right for the junction of my thighs. "Are you always ready for me?"

"Pretty much," I say shakily.

Two knowing fingers go directly to my clit and rub against the ultra-sensitive gathering of nerves. My eyes slide shut. My head tilts back. With a quick jerk of my lace panties, he has me bare and wanton. I see that my burly man has a method to his madness; delicate lace panties tear easily, especially when they're damp. No wonder the dresser is stocked with so many, the dirty scoundrel. I love it. He grips my waist and lifts me to sit on the bathroom vanity. My heart pounds in my chest. I know he's frustrated and this is meant to bring relief. He isn't going to make slow love to me. He's going to fuck me hard and fast and I'm ready for it.

"Who keeps this sweet pussy wet, Josephine?" His words and breath against my cheek elicit an all over shiver.

"You do," I say softly.

His long fingers slide into my depths, furthering my need for him to fill me. "And do you know why this pussy stays wet for me, Josephine?" His fingers glide over my inner walls three, four, five times before he pulls them out. I shake my head no. He pops the two fingers covered in my arousal into his mouth and hums delightfully as he sucks them clean.

"Because..." He unbuttons and unzips his suit pants freeing his erection. It twitches and juts outward in my direction.

"This..." He slowly hitches my dress up around my waist.

I glance down, and the sight of his wide tip grazing against my waiting opening makes my body ache for him.

"Is..." He holds the shaft of his cock with one hand and slides the head of it up then back down my seam. He comes to a stop at the opening to my body, amber eyes lifting to meet mine.

"Mine!" he bellows as he surges forward into me.

I cry out. No amount of sex with him can ever prepare me for the fullness of him. He pauses for just long enough for me to draw in the breath that his power forced from me. His hands grip my hips so hard that I'm sure he'll leave marks. I wrap my legs high on his waist, allowing him the access he demands. The veins in his neck bulge and throb with his accelerated pulse, his eyes clouded with passion. I feel him pull out of me, and every ridge and vein of his shaft sliding deliciously over my inner walls. He plummets back in deep, the wide tip of him jabbing at my insides and sending zaps of pleasure and pain through me. He sets a manic pace, a rhythm of womb-jarring penetration. My hands cling to his muscular shoulder and he dives deep, over and over and over again. With each plunge and withdrawal I am driven towards release. I peek down appreciatively at the erotic beauty of our bodies joined together. The sight of my lips accommodating his wide girth sends a new wave of heat to my center, speeding my pulse even further. He holds me tightly to him and cups my ass to lift me from the counter. I am pressed to him, chest to chest, as he walks us to the wall.

"Hold on tight, baby," he warns and I have zero doubt that I should obey him. I cling hard to him. He pins me between the hard barrier of his chest and the wall. His torso has me blissfully trapped, his hands splayed across my ass. The pain of his short nails digging into my soft flesh is welcome. He pulls his hips from mine, dragging his heavy cock out of me. He drives back in, impaling me hard and fast. His motions continue, unrelentingly. I gasp and dig my nails into his back. His growls and grunts of pleasure are the only sounds to be heard, other than the moist slapping of our bodies colliding. I am completely breathless and euphoric. Abruptly, my body begins the familiar tightening and jolting as the most sudden orgasm topples over me.

"Ah, Damon!" I scream his name and my vision turns distorted and spotty. Air hisses through his gritted teeth. He charges forward once again and stills, planted deep in me.

"Fuck!" he shouts as his body quakes and his cock twitches within me.

His release fills me with new warmth and I revel in the sensation.

"Never leave me, please," he mumbles.

His plea rouses me from my revelry and I realize just how scared he truly is of losing me. Shit, maybe he's just as scared of loss as I am.

I smooth his hair through my fingers. "Why are you scared of losing me? I'm not going anywhere. My heart is yours. I couldn't leave if I tried."

He leans forward and rests his forehead against my shoulder. "Just, never leave."

"I'm not."

I feel his body relax considerably, and all at once I realize that his fear isn't because of me. His mother abandoned him as an infant. That's to be the reason he is so scared of losing me. My big, tough man has mommy issues. Fuck. No wonder he sees Dr. Versan.

He pulls away from me and the ebbing orgasm and adrenaline leaves me with an aching back and a throbbing vagina. I tiptoe to recover my panties, as if walking lightly will somehow ease my achiness. I glance at Damon and he looks apologetic. Shoot. I have to get better at hiding my occasional discomfort when he's rough. Seeing him regretful and sad is far more painful than my minor, temporary pain.

"Don't look like that, I'm fine."

"No, you aren't. I should know better than to touch you when I'm so upset. I hurt my woman."

He steps over to me and pulls me into him, exactly where I like to be. Chest to chest, my head against his heart.

"I'm fine. I love you."

"I love you more than you know."

I smile; with my cheek pressed against his chest, I can hear his heart thump thump. This is the good life, right here.

"I hate that I have to leave you alone, but I have some business to handle."

Opportunity! I wonder if Grams is around to talk...

"It's no problem, I was thinking about going to the grocery store." I smooth my dress down and head for the closet and new panties. I turn to see Damon behind me, scowling. "What?"

"You don't need to shop. I pay someone to do it for us."

Us. That's nice.

"That's such a huge waste of money, Damon. I can go to the store, I have the rest of the day free. I'm going to lose my mind if Hemingway and I are stuck here doing nothing."

He digs out his wallet and flips it open. "Here. Go buy some shit for Hemi or for yourself. Or...whatever."

Here we go with the money issue. He shoves a credit card in my face and the name on it catches my eye. What? I snatch it from his hand and hold it so close it touches my nose, to be sure that I'm not seeing shit.

"This is my name!" I hold up the plastic card accusingly.

"Yes. You're my girlfriend. I plan on keeping you forever. We live together. You need access to funds. So there it is." My jaw hangs open and just like that, I've lost the battle. Again. He steps forward and closes my mouth with one finger pressed to my chin, then kisses me tenderly. "I love you, woman. You and the fur kid stay out of trouble. I'll be home in a couple hours."

He walks out of the big ass closet that now has all my junk on one side. I look down at my feet and there's

Hemingway, who licks his little puppy mouth, effectively reminding me that my "fur kid" needs food.

"What are we going to do with our guy, Hemingway? He's a mystery. Answers are what we need." I scoop up my little guy and head towards the kitchen, but not before grabbing my cell phone. I'll call Grams. She should be able to shed some light.

Chapter Twenty-Four

Coming Apart

I pick up my cell phone and dial Grams while absentmindedly watching Hemingway scarf down his puppy chow.

"Hello?"

"Hey, Grams, it's Jo."

"Hello! I'm so glad you called. I'm sorry about that son of mine. I swear, he enjoys embarrassing me as a mother."

I click my tongue at her apology. "He's a grown ass man, Grams. Let him act stupid if he wants, that's not on you. Hey, I was wondering if you had a minute to chat?"

"Sure. Anything for my supplier."

I laugh out loud; our circus peanut exchanges really are reminiscent of a drug drop, and here I am, enabling an old lady to lose her teeth.

"So, I was wondering about Damon's mother. What's the story? Like, the whooole story."

She sighs knowingly and I can tell she is going to give up the goods. "Well, I guess you'll find out sooner or later. Damon's mother was young. Very young. Edward was already married and had a baby on the way with my now ex-daughter-in-law. Well, from what I know, Eddie was fooling around with this young girl and got her pregnant. With Damon. Her name was Beverly; I don't remember the last name, but I do remember her first name was Beverly. Anyhow, Eddie was awful to her and once Damon was born, she showed up to my house, since by then, Eddie had separated from his wife and he was living at home with me. There he was; a tiny baby boy wrapped in a blue blanket. Said his name was Damon, and he was all ours. Said she was too poor and young and couldn't stand the sight of Damon. I've never told him that part, so keep that to yourself, if you please. It doesn't surprise me, though. I heard the way Eddie spoke to her on the phone once, he is a shameless man. I wasn't going to let him treat my grandson the way he treated that poor girl, so I made him do the right thing and raise his son. My daughter-in-law divorced him as soon as she found out about it all, the hell with trying to reconcile. She left town with my granddaughter and she hasn't had anything to do with Eddie since. I can't blame her."

My mouth hangs wide open and I hear Grams let out a long, sad sigh. My poor, poor Damon.

"I can't believe...I'm so shocked. No wonder you sent him to see Dr. Versan when he was a teenager. He must have been dealing with a lot. With a drunk for a dad and his mom leaving him like that."

She lets out another sigh. "Well, actually, that's a whole other tragic story. He started seeing Versan after the accident."

Accident? What accident? He's never talked about any accident. He knows about my accident, but has never once talked about himself being involved in one.

"So, why exactly did he need Versan after the accident?" Please keep talking. Please keep talking. I can hear her take a deep breath and I know she's hesitant to say anymore.

"Honey you have to understand. He was only seventeen when that horrible thing happened and he couldn't quite handle it."

"Handle what?"

"He and Eddie were arguing and they crashed head-on into a family."

My heart seizes in my chest and all at once familiarity hits me like a shotgun blast.

"When did this happen?" My eyes lock onto a spot on the floor and I can't tear them away. My focus is completely consumed with Grams' story.

"Back in June of '96, I believe. The mother and father were killed. There was a little girl that Damon pulled out of the car, but we never knew what happened to her. I think she made it, but when we searched for information about her we were held up at every turn. Red tape with the foster system and all. Damon never got over it, he said the little girl broke his heart. She was screaming for her parents and covered in blood. He said he knew they had passed, but just held the girl to him and carried her away from it. Don't you understand, honey? He blames himself for the accident, for killing those poor people."

My eyes bulge and my heart squeezes. "I have to go." I hang up before she can respond. My eyes stare off into space while I try to focus on breathing. He killed my parents. The man I am in love with killed my parents. He took Maman and Papa from me. My entire fucking life has been hell because of him. I hate him. I hate him almost as much as I love him and being split like this is a hell I wouldn't wish on anyone.

Do something. Anything. I snap out of my trance and look down at Hemingway. I scoop him up and jog upstairs to the bedroom. I set him on the bed and hurry into the closet. I grab a box and begin packing. I can't stay here. I can't be with him. The moment I think of it, my heart breaks into a million pieces in my chest. I bend down and gather a heap of clothes into my arms and throw them back into the box they came from. I toss things in haphazardly then head to the bathroom to do the same. I gather up all of Hemingway's shit and pack it in a hurry. One by one, I carry the boxes down to the big, gray sedan I inherited from Captain. I can't believe I'm leaving. I don't want to leave. But, I have to leave. He killed my parents, for God's sake. He knew who the fuck I was! He had to have known. The thought of him knowing and keeping it hidden has my blood boiling. I do one more pass through the penthouse to see if I missed anything important. I search for my mother's watch but it's nowhere to be found. Damnit! I load my puppy into his carrier and leave.

I arrive at Sutton's house and hesitate as I turn the lock and walk in. Deep breath. I'm ready for this. There are still plastic wrappers on the floor from the sterilized medical supplies that the paramedics used on him. I set Hemingway's carrier down and collapse in a heap. I sob and sob. I cry for the loss of my parents; for Sutton, my Captain; for falling in love with a man who is my absolute other half and forfeiting him to circumstance. I pound my fist hard on the floor, sharp pain radiating through my arm.

"Please, not Damon. Not him," I cry out to no one. Tears course down my heated face. My eyes swell and burn, but it's nothing compared to the torture I'm feeling inside. I've betrayed the memory of my parents by falling in love with the person responsible for their death. I can never forgive myself. I ache for Damon, too. When he discovers what I know, and that I've left, he's going to lose it. I don't want to hurt him like his mother hurt him. I love him too much to ever cause him pain.

"Damnit!" I have to go see him. I have to try to explain why I can't be with him anymore and I need answers. I need to know if everything was a big lie. If what we have is a lie...

When I enter the high rise, I look to Howard and hear him talking on the phone at his desk.

"She just walked in now, Boss."

I don't even acknowledge him as I walk right to the elevators. I rub my miserable eyes and take a deep breath. The doors ding and slide open.

"Here we go," I mumble to myself as I step out into the main foyer. I punch in the code and open the door, walking into the room on unsteady legs. My hands are shaking uncontrollably. I can feel my lip quivering and I don't bother trying to hide my emotion. I let it flow, uninhibited; the hell with my normal self control.

He's waiting for me. I feel him in the room.

"You knew."

Damon's gaze snaps to me and without saying a word, I know that I'm right. The sorrow and regret I see in his eyes crashes down on me like the heaviest of burdens.

"No. No." I'm shaking my head, begging for words of denial from him, but he says nothing.

He stands and starts towards me, but I reflexively begin backing away as he advances.

"No. Not you, Damon." My voice cracks through my quiet sobs.

"Josephine. Baby, listen to me."

"NO! Don't you fucking call me that!"

He stops in his tracks and runs his hands through his dark, mussed hair. Part of me wants to wrap my arms around the man that I love so completely, but the wounded part of me wants nothing more than to make him hurt like I have hurt for sixteen long, miserable years. We stare at each other for a moment. What the fuck am I supposed to do with this? I fell in love with the man who killed my family. He let me fall for him. He knew who I was, and he never said a word. He swept me off my feet. He made me want him. Then he made me need him and now I can't imagine my life without him. I love him more than my next breath. I need him more than my next breath.

"Jo, I wanted to tell you. I tried to tell you. Damnit, you have to believe me, Baby."

"How long? How long have you known?" My voice is a small whisper, but menacing at the same time.

Damon's amber eyes are no longer warm and inviting. They look tormented and empty as they shift about. His chest deflates and I'm torn between gathering him into my arms and attacking him with my claws.

"When you gave me your e-mail address at the coffee shop, I thought I recognized the name. I checked to be sure. Then the watch, I remembered seeing it on your mom's wrist when I checked her pulse. I found the scar on your leg and confirmed it. I knew it was you."

That's why he was all weird about my scar? He knew it was from the accident. He verified my identity while we were intimate for the first time?

"You son of a bitch. You saw the scar and the watch that proved who I am and you still fucked me? Or maybe that's why you fucked me. In reality, it's probably the only reason I'm here right now. Right? Trying to make it right? Trying to shower me with your money and your gifts so that you can call it even? So that causing the death of my parents won't feel as shitty? I'm a fucking charity case.

That's what this is. You don't love me, you're trying to settle the score. You have no fucking shame and I can't stand the sight of you."

I knew my words had to hurt him because they tore through me as I said them. I don't want to believe a single word. I don't believe that he doesn't love me. I can't. But, my judgment is distorted. This is so fucked up. It's more awful than my worst nightmare.

"Please, let's try to figure this out. You're my everything, Josephine, you're my world. I need you." He starts moving toward me again and I put my hand out, halting him in his tracks.

"Yeah, well I don't need or want you. I hate you, Damon," I lie. God, how I lie. I need and want him more than I can express. Words fail me in the worst way when I try to think of ways to describe how much I love him.

I turn in place and will my numb body to carry me away from this place as fast as it can. By some miracle, I find myself speed-walking back to the door. I know Damon is hot on my trail, I can feel him near me like I always do. His fingers clasp the crook of my elbow and spin me to face him. I wrench myself from his grip.

"Don't touch me!" I practically growl.

Damon's face is one of complete despair and I ache even more at the sight of it. I can't believe God would be so unfair. Why in the world would I be put through this? It isn't fair. I've lost everything. I love a man that I can't possibly allow myself to have. He's the reason my life has been so awful. He knew the truth and hid it from me. He sinks to his knees in front of me and my heart clenches in my chest so hard that I think I may be having a heart attack. His head hangs down and he stares at the ground. I stand here, wishing that I could change everything. I wish I could be his and he mine, but it just isn't possible. I hate life for doing this to me.

"Please. Let me explain," he mumbles, and I see tears dropping from his eyes onto the tile floor. He can't even look at me. My lip quivers and I'm dying a thousand deaths watching the scene of my strong man kneel in defeat.

"I can't." I force out the words and hate that I even said them. But what other option do I have? Anything I feel for him pales in comparison to the grief that I will always feel for the loss of my parents and the years of hell that loss precipitated. I turn to leave, knowing I'm killing both of us, but I can't look at the man who took my parents from me so long ago. I slam his front door with such force that I startle. Even through the heavy door and walls, I hear Damon coming undone at the seams. I ignore the animalistic yelling and crashing noises and all but run to

Sutton's car. Damnit! I don't want to leave him like that. The idea of him hurting sends my heart into a fit, but I have no choice. I have to get out of here and sort my head out before I do anything else.

Chapter Twenty-Five

Best and Worst

My phone rang off the hook until I turned it off completely. He pounded on my door until that snobby neighbor called the damned police to have him removed. I haven't checked my email. I haven't gone anywhere. I haven't done...anything. Nothing. I have been lucky to even exist right here on Sutton's old sofa. Four days. That's how long it's been since I last saw Damon. Four days since my entire world fell apart. I wonder if this shit will ever feel any better. The way it feels now, I highly doubt it. A banging on the door gets Hemingway yipping his tiny bark and I groan like a dying animal. I feel like a dying animal.

"Goooo awaaaaaaaay!"

The banging gets louder.

"Girl, you better open this door!" GRAMS! Oh shit, Grams! She'll have a heart attack in this heat. I roll off the couch and crawl on fours for a beat before finally standing up and swinging the door open with such a rush that a hot gust of air travels in with it.

Grams takes one look at me and nearly chokes. "You look like shit! I mean real shit! A big steaming pile—"

"I get it! Come in, Grams."

She smiles politely and looks over her shoulder to a waiting car and holds up a shaky finger. She shuffles in with her walker, tennis balls and all.

"I came to set you right, young lady!"

Set me right? What the fuck? I screw my face all up and she wrinkles her nose at me. I guess it's not my best look.

"Me?"

"Yep! You!" she says sternly, wagging a finger menacingly at me. "As much as it pains me, I have to set you straight."

It pains her? Awesome. I guess she doesn't like me as much as I like her.

"I love you to pieces. I hope that once you hear what I have to say, you'll go find Damon and you two will kiss and makeup."

"What do you mean, go find him?" Where the hell is he? My heart speeds and I panic a bit. The thought of never seeing him again is one that has me frantic.

J.L. Mac

"I'll get to that in a minute. One thing at a time."

I nod and do my best to appear calm and attentive.

"So, he had two letters delivered to me today. One was for me and one was for you. In my letter, he said he knew you would come see me at some point and he wanted me to give it to you. But first and foremost, you have to know that Damon wasn't driving."

"What?!" I screech.

She shakes her head from side to side. "He was not driving. My drunk, lousy, no good son was. He made Damon tell the police that it was him who wrecked the car because he was a minor and mostly, because he wasn't drunk. Damon has always blamed himself because he couldn't get Eddie to pullover and let him drive."

Oh, no. I lean forward clutch my aching stomach. I feel like I may be ill. He didn't do it. It's not his fault. "How could he think...How... It's not his fault." I cross the room and sit beside Grams. She puts my shaking hand in hers and lets me sob for a moment.

"I have to see him. I have to talk to him!" I begin looking around for car keys then she thrusts out an envelope to me.

"He isn't answering and no one knows where he is. Open your letter maybe he has told you where he went." I snatch the envelope from her hand and rip it open.

My Josephine,

I should have been smarter that day, I should have been braver. I should have stopped him at all costs. If I had, maybe none of this ever would have happened. You never would have been hurt. We could have met and spent our lives together. You must know that I have spent countless days thinking of how I could have changed the outcome of that summer day so long ago. Had I known how things would turn out, I would have done anything to spare you and your family from the tragedy for which I hold myself responsible. He wrecked more than cars that day. He wrecked your life and mine in the process. And I was the only one who could have stopped it all. I would take their place if I could. I would do anything that would bring you happiness. I will make sure that I am but a memory to you. You won't have to endure the pain of seeing me again. The anguish I saw in your eyes four days ago was far more than I could ever bare. I can only hope that perhaps, one day, you will be able to look back on us and smile, recalling the passion and love we shared. Those are memories that torment and comfort me, all at the same time. When you were mine, you made everything better. You made my life better. You made me better. You have been my medicine. You made the hurt disappear. My past is one that I can never escape, I know this now. Please know that I would do anything, I would give anything, to make things right. I want to thank you for giving me the greatest gift I have ever known. For what seems like a fleeting moment, I lived in the bliss of your affection. To never know that bliss again is an agony that I cannot endure. My heart is forever yours, Josephine. I love you.

    -Damon

    PS. You get it all.

My eyes bulge and water. What does he mean he won't see me again? What does he mean I get it all? Get all of what? My heart pounds so hard in my chest I can barely breathe. Grams pulls the letter from my hand and reads it. I jump from my seat and start searching for shoes. I grab the nearest pair of sandals and strip down right there in the living room in front of her. I pull a clean shirt over my head and shorts up my legs. Where would he be? I have no clue where to even start.

"The accident," she mutters while staring down at the letter.

"What?"

Her silver haired head lifts to me and I see tears swimming in her eyes. "The scene of that accident. He used to go there and park along the shoulder to sit. He'd sit there for hours until I would come find him. You have to go get him."

Without hesitation, I grab keys from the coffee table and run out the door. I jump from the top step to the bottom and nearly bust my ass on the walkway. I scurry to Sutton's car and start the beast up. I know where the scene is, I've been there a thousand times, too. I used to go sit there and be miserable, thinking about Maman and Papa and the boy who pulled me from that car. I thought of Damon all these years. He's been in my head for so many years. I never forgot the big boy who kept saying how sorry he was and that he would make sure I was okay. He did, too. He made sure I was more than okay. He found me again that day in the bookstore and it's like everything changed in an instant. I have to find him. I have to tell him that it's not his fault. I have to tell him how much I love him.

I speed and drive carelessly to the outskirts of town. When I turn onto the familiar, narrow road, my heart aches in my chest. A terrible knot forms in my stomach. Something is wrong. Something is wrong. I know it. I can feel it, like I felt it when Sutton died. My foot bares down on the gas and the car surges forward even faster. I haul ass down the road until I see tail lights come into focus. I lean forward in my seat and squint.

"The truck!" I drive up behind the truck and come screeching to a halt, kicking up dust in the process. I throw the car in park and jump out. I can't see him sitting in there. There's no one in the fucking truck! Where could he be? I run up to the truck and climb up on the running board to peek in.

"Damon!" I gasp and jump down. I jerk the door open and the scent of alcohol smacks me in the face.

"Damon! Baby, wake up!"

I climb into the truck and use every ounce of strength I have to lift him from his position laying across the seat. I manage to get him upright and then realize that the best news just turned into the worst. In his lifeless hand is a prescription bottle.

"Oh shit! Oh shit! What did you do?" I scream out. I jump from the truck and run back to the car.

"Come on. Come on. Come on." I find my phone and call for help. I don't even wait for the dispatcher to say anything.

"Please help! We're on Scenic Loop! There's been an accident. Send an ambulance!" I run back to the truck and jump in.

"Oh, please, baby! Baby, wake up!" I slap his face a few times, but he doesn't respond. I thrust out two fingers and hold them to his neck, then to his wrist.

"No. No. No. Damon!" I lay his heavy, limp body across my lap and rock back and forth.

"Please no! Not you. Don't leave me. Don't leave me. I love you! Please, Damon!" He doesn't respond and I fear that he is really gone. This is my fault. The guilt is immediate and crushing. This must be how he has felt for years. My poor Damon! My lip quivers as tears pour from my eyes.

I hear the ambulance arrive and doors slamming.

"Ma'am, we need you to move now."

I slip from under him and his unresponsive body lay in the seat. A police officer grabs me up and drags me back.

"Damon! Please! Wake up!" I watch helplessly as they pull his body from his truck and lay him on a stretcher. One paramedic straddles his body and starts resuscitation efforts. The other two haul the gurney into the back of the ambulance with the one paramedic still working on Damon.

I met him right in this very spot under horrible circumstances so many years ago and now, I may have lost him in this same spot. I can't lose him. I could never survive a life without Damon. I fall to my knees and the pain of the pavement beneath them isn't even a blip on the radar compared to the ache in my chest. I watch the flashing lights of the ambulance fade into the distance. I remain staring, paralyzed with shock and fear. I can't lose him. I've only just found him.

Stay Connected with J. L. Mac

Twitter: http://twitter.com/JaimiLMcCormick

Facebook: www.facebook.com/jlmacbooks

Blog: http://jlmacbooks.blogspot.com/

Acknowledgements

Whoever said that road rage precipitates nothing but bad things? I would have to disagree. Wreck Me was conceived of Hulk like road rage and asshat holiday drivers. This story was born amidst dense traffic, a barrage of swear words, some less than civilized sign language, and honking horns. I would like to give a particularly big thanks to the jerk-wad in the Mitsubishi. Thanks for the inspiration you stop sign running penis wrinkle!

Aside from the above mentioned joker, and my Hulk tendencies, I have to attribute my determination to my many friends, fellow authors, and bloggers. You all are simply incredible. I could not and would not be a writer without the support you give so selflessly.

Justin, love of my life. Handsome charming man of mine. I love you with a wholeness that is incomprehensible. Any efforts of defining the depth of my love and adoration with words are simply futile. They all fall short.

About the Author

J.L. Mac is twenty-six years old and currently resides in El Paso, Texas, where she enjoys living near her parents and siblings. She was born and raised in Galveston, Texas, until she married her husband in July of 2005. She has two young children and is married to a soldier in the United States Army. J.L. and her family have lived all over the United States and have enjoyed each new experience in each new place. J.L. admittedly has had a long and sordid love affair with the written word and has loved every minute of it.

She drinks too many glasses of wine on occasion, and says way too many swear words to be considered "lady-like." J.L. spends her free time reading, writing, and playing with her children.